MURDER IN THE MAZE

The village of Redingote anticipated the usual misbehavior during the annual summer fête. But no one expected murder . . .

FROZEN STIFF

The new management consultant at Tesbury's grocery chain has annoyed a lot of people with his meddling. Now he's made someone angry enough to commit murder . . .

CORPSE IN THE KITCHEN

She was baking bread—until an unknown party turned the staff of life into the stuff of death . . . and choked her with a wad of raw dough. Now the heat is on Trewley and Stone . . .

DYING BREATH

Dr. Holbrook was a brilliant scientist—until somebody made him the guinea pig for an experiment in murder . . .

SEW EASY TO KILL

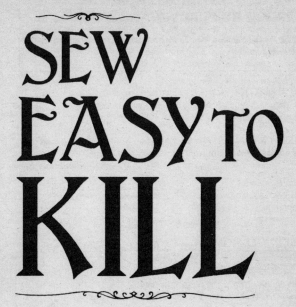

Sarah J. Mason

BERKLEY PRIME CRIME, NEW YORK

SEW EASY TO KILL

A Berkley Prime Crime Book / published by arrangement with the author

PRINTING HISTORY
Berkley Prime Crime edition / May 1996

The Putnam Berkley World Wide Web site address is
http://www.berkley.com

ISBN: 0-425-15310-X

Berkley Prime Crime Books are published by
The Berkley Publishing Group,
200 Madison Avenue, New York, NY 10016.
The name BERKLEY PRIME CRIME and the BERKLEY PRIME CRIME
design are trademarks belonging to Berkley Publishing Corporation.

PRINTED IN THE UNITED STATES OF AMERICA

10 9 8 7 6 5 4 3 2 1

One

THE LITTLE ROOM had but one occupant. Behind his desk, a heavy, thickset man lay slumped in the padded chair. His head was thrown back, lolling motionless against the pale green distemper of the wall; on the incongruous pink of his blotter, a solitary white shirt button, torn threads still attached, bore witness to some recent act of violence in the region of the man's neck, where his tie hung askew with a distorted knot, and the collar gaped wide about his throat.

The man—even half-hidden by the desk he gave an impression of brooding bulk—did not move. Through the open window, the song of a distant bird was drowned out by the rumble of approaching cars; the very faintest of breezes stirred the bulky one's brown hair and whispered among the topmost papers on his desk.

That whisper, like every other sound to be heard in the little room, went unheeded.

Footsteps pattered in the corridor outside and came to a halt at the door. There was a quick, breathless fumbling at the handle . . . and a young woman—slim, dark-haired, alert—paused on the threshold with a large cardboard box in her arms.

She stared for a moment at the motionless man before her. The lines and deep furrows on his face—giving him the appearance of a bulldog, or perhaps a bloodhound—hinted at much past suffering.

She coughed. She took a few tentative steps into the room. She coughed again.

The man, still without moving, groaned. The young woman grinned. The man groaned again, opened one eye, and rolled it desperately in the direction of the new arrival. He saw what she carried, forced open his other eye, and struggled more or less upright.

"You got it, then." He almost smiled. "Good girl." His voice dropped to a growl as relief gave way to apprehension. "Uh—did he see you?"

"Come off it, sir. Would I be in one piece if he had?" Detective Sergeant Stone dumped the box on her desk, dusted her hands, and favoured her superior with a decidedly scornful look. "You know as well as I do that theories of equal rank are neither here nor there for Sergeant Pleate when it comes to raids on his precious Lost Property cupboard. He'd have had me on a charge and busted down to meter maid if he'd so much as blinked at me."

Detective Superintendent Trewley had to acknowledge the truth of this. Thoughtfully, he rubbed his lugubrious chin. "Well, with any luck he won't find out, if we're quick about it." He sighed. "But then, if he does . . ."

"I'll tell him it's nothing to do with me," came Stone's prompt reply. "I was just obeying orders." She launched into a Humphrey Bogart imitation. "Don't be too sure I'm as crooked as I'm supposed to be, sweetheart. I'm not taking the rap for you!" In her normal voice, she added, "After all, if he's going to turn one or other of us into mincemeat, sir—well, you're a lot more used to it than I am."

This truth, likewise, was undeniable. Desk Sergeant Pleate had long viewed the entire Allingham police station as his own particular kingdom. He brooked no rebellion, even from his nominal commander: the authority of a mere superintendent counted for nothing against the power of the iron truncheon with which the sergeant ruled his numerous troops. In matters of basic discipline, Trewley was inclined to accept that Pleate had a point. The Allingham force was, without doubt, the best in Allshire, as the most impartial observer must agree. Superintendent Trewley was far from being impartial, but he would always give credit where credit was due.

What he was never, at any time, prepared to give was his blessing to Pleate's perpetual claim that it was in the best interests of maximum efficiency for items of Lost Property to be retained by the police for as long as three calendar months before disposal. Trewley's contention, every time this thorny topic was raised, was that a period of one month ought really to be enough; but Pleate turned a resolutely deaf ear to his superior's protests, and an elaborately made key in the lock of the cupboard. If the cupboard ran out of shelf space, the sergeant would smartly annexe one of the less popular interview rooms before anyone found out, dropping loud hints about permanent quarters which would drive Trewley wild.

It was the lock of this appropriated interview room that Detective Sergeant Stone had—with a skeleton key and a thumping heart—just successfully picked.

"Let's see what we've got." Her pocketknife sawed at the tape sealing the heavy carton on her desk. Sticky fragments collected particles of cardboard dust as they drifted to the floor. Trewley looked on with hopeful interest, running an anguished hand inside his collar and finally wrenching off his loosened tie, thereby completing the ruin which had first inspired his sergeant to rush off on her illicit errand of mercy. "I was scared stiff he'd catch me, so I didn't waste time checking inside, but . . ." Stone lifted the flap and pulled back the lid of the inner box. "I've a nasty suspicion . . . Yes. Bother," she said as she reached in and removed her prize. "I was right. No plug."

Trewley sat up and glowered. "Which only goes to show just how long he must've had the blasted thing tucked away in there. Three months be damned—three years, more like! Isn't everything electric supposed to be fitted with a plug before you buy it nowadays?"

"I'm not going back there after a plug." Obedience to command was all very well, but . . . "Once was once too often. My nerves may never be the same again."

"All in a good cause, my girl, remember that."

"Good for whom, sir? Not for me. A true self-sacrifice on my part . . ." But her reply was half-hearted as she cast a contemplative eye around the office. For some moments there was renewed silence as she pondered, watched hopefully by her superior. At last, with a brisk nod, she dropped suddenly to the floor and began wriggling her arm sideways behind the tall filing cabinet in the corner. "If you *had* gone and died of heat exhaustion," she remarked as she wriggled, "I'd have been a good step nearer promotion than—ah! Got it."

There came a click from the back of the cabinet, followed by a metallic clunk and a muffled oath. "Tight fit," said Stone as she scrambled to her feet, trailing a long, black, electric flex from the plastic plug in her hand. "We won't use that particular socket again, if you don't mind. I should think I've broken every bone in my wrist getting the plug out."

"As long as you haven't broken the plug." Trewley wiped his forehead with a large polka-dot handkerchief, closed his eyes, and exhaled with vigour. "It's not as if we use the projector that much, I suppose. . . . Put your skates on, girl. Or are you trying to make it *Inspector* Stone a bit too quick for my liking?"

"Perish the thought, sir." Stone was rummaging in her desk. "Good. I thought I hadn't thrown these away." From the back of the bottom drawer she retrieved a small pair of scissors with one broken blade. "You never know when things will come in handy. . . . And the whatsit on my penknife should do for a screwdriver. Hang on just a bit longer, sir. I think rescue may be imminent."

Trewley hung on as instructed, leaning back in his chair and welcoming the smooth coolness of the wall against his neck and scalp. He uttered a loan moan, and again rubbed his face with his handkerchief.

Stone ignored him as she set to work with penknife and improvised screwdriver-scissors, separating the two halves of the slide projector plug, slackening the clip that held the flex, and releasing the copper terminal wires from live and neutral. "So far, so good . . ."

But it was her turn to be ignored. She addressed herself instead to her Lost Property plunder, using scissors to strip away from the flex both the outer and inner casings for a length of two inches before at last fastening the old plug to the new appliance, and sitting back with a sigh of satisfaction.

"All done. Where do you want it?" She frowned, brushing her hair out of her face. "On top of the filing cabinet is the most efficient place, of course, but without using an extension lead there's no convenient socket. I haven't a clue where the lead has gone—and this is no time to start shoving furniture around."

"I didn't say a word."

"I know you didn't, sir."

"Umph." Trewley opened two accusing eyes and sat up. "My wife been getting at you about my blood pressure again, has she?"

The charge was less incongruous than it might at first have seemed. Before becoming a police officer, Stone had hoped to serve the community by entering medical college, for which she'd been academically more than qualified; but the discovery that she found it almost impossible to accept the reality of blood forced her to abandon the course. Medicine's loss had been the superintendent's gain, though he would never tell her so: he didn't hold with letting his youthful subordinate get above herself, even if he would occasionally, in private, admit that they made a good team.

"Blood pressure's nothing to do with it," Stone said now. "Any doctor would say it's far too hot for people, whether or not they have weight problems"—Trewley glared—"to go in for anything, um, physical when it isn't strictly necessary. Not by themselves, that is," she qualified, with an appraising look at the cabinet in question. "On the other hand, failing an extension lead, if we could rustle up a few chaps with a bit of beef . . ."

"I suppose young What's-His-Name might do." For whimsical reasons of his own, Trewley always professed himself unable to remember the name of the Traffic officer with whom Sergeant Stone shared her private life. "At a pinch. If he's not out on his rounds terrorising innocent motorists." He hadn't the energy to chuckle. "And then Benson or Hedges could always be hiding somewhere. . . ."

Stone decided that he was in no fit state to telephone the duty room, and made the call herself. She didn't waste time on details; she enquired after PC Benson, heard that he was in the canteen, and at once volunteered—since the canteen lay in the opposite direction to the desk of Sergeant Pleate—to pop along and fetch that keen young man and his enduringly taciturn colleague to perform an errand of mercy for their anguished chief.

And within five minutes, to the satisfaction of all concerned—and to the immense relief of the tormented Trewley—the electric fan, liberated from its long Lost Property imprisonment, was oscillating merrily from one side of the room to the other; and the temperature, after hours of stifling heat, was almost bearable again.

"Sometimes," said Gladys Franklin, "I wonder how much more of all this I can bear." Fanning herself with the sheet of paper in her free hand, the needlework teacher sighed gustily across the telephone mouthpiece. "I do so like to think of myself as being a . . . a positive person, Mrs. Humphries, but I really can't remember when we last had such appalling weather, can you? That thunderstorm the other day did absolutely nothing to help. And such a—a great civic responsibility makes it so much harder for me than for . . . well, for others to cope with. As I'm sure you understand."

Allingham Town Hall's Mrs. Humphries was quick to commiserate with the unhappy teacher: she'd had a lot of practice in commiserating over recent weeks. While an English summer might be generally regarded as a damp, grey, dismal three months leavened by rare days (seldom at the weekend) of brilliant sunshine, this year had seen a startling exception to the rule. Weather professionals had pontificated in the press, drawn diagrams for television, and rambled on the radio about the unusually stable area of high pressure that appeared to have taken up residence above the British Isles. For more than three weeks now, Brighton had been hotter than Barcelona, London than Lisbon, Manchester than Madrid. There were rumours of a hosepipe ban. Sales of portable air conditioners, electric fans, and chemicals for domestic swimming pools quadrupled. Umbrella manufacturers, fearing bankruptcy, had bought vast quantities of lace and ribbon to transform their profitless stock into parasols. Supermarkets did a roaring trade in soft drinks and ice cream; ice-cream salesmen badgered suppliers for additional vans, and their triumphant summoning chimes drowned out the nation's songbirds from dawn till dusk.

Burglars were taking unfair advantage of opened windows; insurance companies were employing extra staff to write letters denying liability. Fire brigades issued warnings about carelessness with matches. The nation's butchers beamed as sales of bacon, sausages, steak, and kebab skewers rose in direct proportion to the number of barbecues sold. Osteopaths reported increased numbers of patients with disks damaged by deck-chair lounging; doctors treated sunburn in the most surprising places. Bald men bought panama hats; men with heavy beards began, in desperation, to have serious thoughts about razors. . . .

"If only," Gladys lamented as Judith Humphries ran out of soothing things to say, "we could all have a good night's sleep, it wouldn't be so bad. But when there's no air, the way it's been, it's simply impossible—and nobody can concentrate on their work or keep their temper day after day if they haven't slept. The children have turned into thorough-going little monsters, and in a way one can hardly blame them. And as for my evening class—"

"Yes, your evening class." Judith was quick to cut in as Gladys at last returned to the topic about which she'd first phoned more than ten minutes earlier. "Are you saying there's a problem? Would you rather cancel your contribution for this year? It will be a *little* awkward, of course, with only a fortnight to go—but I do know what a pride you take in your pupils' work, and I quite understand that you don't want to let yourself, or them, down by submitting anything of inferior quality for public display. Please don't worry, Mrs. Franklin," she said as Gladys began to sputter. "I'm sure I'll be able to juggle enough things around to fill—"

"Cancel?" The dismay in those two horrified syllables brought a satisfied smile to the lips of Judith Humphries, safely out of sight in Allingham Town Hall. She'd thought it would work. "*Cancel?* Certainly not! I never said any such thing!"

"Oh, dear, I'm so sorry," said Mrs. Humphries at once. "But I thought you were telling me—"

"I wasn't." Gladys fanned herself again and almost dropped the telephone in her agitation. "What *can* have given you that idea? I was simply explaining that . . . well, that one or two members of my advanced sewing classes are—are somewhat temperamental at the best of times, which one could hardly say this terrible heat wave is. With the result that we may be a little . . . not late, exactly—but not exactly prompt, either, in delivering our finished handiwork to the Town Hall. Perhaps not even until a day or so before the exhibition opens, in fact—yes." Now it was the turn of Gladys Franklin to smile an invisible smile. "Everyone's having to take so much more care, you see, forever rushing off to wash our hands—try as one might, when it's so hot it's impossible not to get a little grubby—and it all takes time, like stopping every few minutes for something to drink, which naturally we can't allow anywhere near the sewing in case of accidents . . ."

"Yes, of course," soothed Mrs. Humphries as further sounds of frantic fanning rustled in her ear. "Everybody knows what pride you all take in your work—and rightly so. The needlecraft exhibits are one of the regular highlights of the show."

Gladys bristled slightly at being, with her pupils, no more than *one* of the highlights of "Allingham in August: An Annual Celebration," but decided that discretion, in the circumstances, was the better part. "I'm glad that's cleared up, then. You'll have them leave our usual number of tables and display stands free—and they won't worry if we don't put in our appearance until almost the last minute?"

Mrs. Humphries injected her sympathy with the merest hint of steel. "As long as you can guarantee that the committee won't be left with nothing on the day itself, I believe we can agree to that—but the afternoon before, at the latest. If you please."

"Yes, yes, I promise." Gladys was still flapping her paper fan. "You're so lucky in the Town Hall. Those thick walls—the high ceilings—those enormous windows . . ."

"Are pretty well useless when there's no breeze. And we aren't so lucky in the winter."

"Oh—well, no. No, I can see it would be less comfortable in the winter—but," she added, sighing, "just now, winter seems such a long way away. . . . I've tried to have my classes moved to the old building, but they say it can't be done—insurance, or some such administrative nonsense, when it's only for a few weeks. As if we couldn't arrange to move a few tables by ourselves! And the janitor is a most helpful young man—but no, we have to stay in the new building, which is fearfully inconvenient. It faces southwest, you know." Her tone became a trifle waspish. "Miss Shorey, I think, would have permitted our removal if it had been left to her, but Miss Thoday was—is—adamant." The wasp grew more like a hornet. "She seems determined to make her presence felt, but I can't help feeling that it might have been wiser for such a very new broom to settle in for a term or two before starting to throw her weight around in such an inconvenient—and unpopular—fashion. . . ."

Mrs. Humphries, a public servant, did not respond to this invitation to pass comment on either the recently installed headmistress, or her disappointed deputy, of the most prestigious and exclusive girls' school in Allingham.

"But there, we can't all be popular," said Mrs. Franklin, buzzing back to normal. "And whatever happens, you may rely on me—on us, Mrs. Humphries. Have we ever let you down in the past?"

"Not once in eight years," said Judith with approval. "And I'm sure you won't this year. Still, thank you for warning me that we needn't expect anything until the Friday; we'll look forward to your contribution as we always do, but just a little later than on previous occasions." She laughed. "Unless, that is, the weather breaks soon enough for your classes to complete their entries by the usual time."

"According to the forecast, it won't. I only wish it would." Gladys gave her loudest sigh so far. "*Temperamental* is an understatement, believe me. Between the two of us, Mrs. Humphries, if it gets any hotter, I won't be at all surprised if—if some people started to turn nasty. . . ."

—————— Two ——————

"SHUT UP! SHUT up, the lot of you! If you don't stop that bleeding row this minute, so help me I'll swing for you!"

Rather than risk it, Julie Garner flung herself, sobbing, out of the room in which her three small children were squabbling, and closed the door with a vicious slam. For one startled moment the screams and squeals were silenced; then they began again. The young Garners were being raised in a tough school.

School! It was the school—St. Catherine's—that was really to blame for Julie's outburst: for most of her recent outbursts, indeed. And they were many, since Craig had lost his job at Allingham Alloys. Poor timekeeping, they'd said. As if she hadn't done her level best to get him off to work in the mornings! But what else did they expect? With the kids keeping themselves awake half the night waiting for him to come home—off down the pub drinking the money away, like as not, with his flash friends she'd never really taken to—and creating a rumpus when she wouldn't let them get up when he did finally condescend to remember he'd a wife and family, waltzing in at all hours with not a care in the world, saying he couldn't see what the fuss was about and she'd no right to expect him to do without his fun when he'd earned it, if anyone had; the rows, and the shouting, and the kids waking up crying and not settling for hours, and Craig yelling at her for being a lousy mother for letting her kids behave so bad . . .

"*My* kids? It takes two, remember? Mine *and* yours, you bastard!" she'd yelled back. And he'd thumped her—thumped her!—and said, well, he wouldn't swear to that, and didn't think she'd want to, either, being as they'd neither of them exactly lived the quiet life before hitching up, and people didn't change, and it was a pity he'd let her play him for a sucker at the time, but there'd been a lot of good men caught that way, and he didn't think he'd be the last. . . .

Oh, he'd apologised next morning, all right, but Julie didn't—couldn't—forget. "Want me to have a bleeding blood test, do you?" she'd thrown at him as he sat, his head in his hands, at the breakfast table, cursing the kids for messing their cereal and spilling their orange juice and acting up the way kids always did, when they knew they could get away with it because their mother was too tired to stop them. Unless she hit them. Or walked out . . .

Except where would she go, if she did? With her dad years gone, her mum married again—and the new bloke *ever* so keen to give his wife's only daughter too many stepfatherly cuddles if she let him. Except that they weren't stepfatherly at all. And if her mum ever found out, she'd say it was Julie's fault for leading him on—as if a man like him ever needed an excuse when he wanted to get inside a girl's knickers! She'd bet he hadn't waited for the registrar to give him the go-ahead for fun and games with his future wife. . . .

Fun? Yeah, for about five minutes—and then you paid for the rest of your life, or what seemed like it. One kid, and responsible for it until it was sixteen; then twins, of all things, ten months later—twice the work, and no fun at all, with her already so tired from the first—and another year longer to pay. Did Craig honestly think anyone with any sense would risk dumping all that on themselves just for a bit of *fun?* What with a mortgage, and the way the kids kept growing—with two after one, you couldn't hand down anywhere near enough shoes and clothes, and even with a sewing machine there was a limit to what she could do. And the little horrors'd fight over sharing their toys soon as look at each other. . . . *Fun*. Oh, chance'd be a fine thing. Three kids, and none at school yet—wouldn't she just love the time for a bit of fun! And never mind the money side of it because if she *did* play around, she'd take good care to pick someone with a full wallet, not just a body and looks that made a girl—all the girls—breathe a bit faster when he was near, and go all hot and funny inside. There was more to life than that. . . .

Not that Craig could see it. Typical man, he liked his fun, and he took it—and her—whenever he wanted, which was why they had three brats and, she was horribly afraid, a fourth starting, because she'd felt sick twice in the bathroom mornings this week, and that's how she'd been with the others, a month gone; and now he'd got this new job— she'd have thought the novelty would wear off after a while, but seemed it still hadn't—he was getting clear of the house as soon as he'd had his breakfast, like he'd done today, and not coming back except sometimes for a quick bite midday, or a cup of tea, leaving her and the kids alone the whole day in this poky little house, all corners and steps and not even a decent kitchen. . . .

The kitchen. Julie had drifted, drying her tears on the sleeve of her faded blouse, away from the tiny lounge where it sounded like World War III was breaking out, along the hall with its uneven tiled floor and that gloomy paint on the doors. Scumbling, they'd called it when they'd given her the guided tour, and she'd been so relieved it looked like Craig would get the caretaker's job after all. Two layers on a wood-grain pattern, done with combs, trying to make out it was better than chipboard—which she'd much rather've had because you could smarten chipboard with gloss and a few transfers, or beading and false panels. . . .

Craig could've done that. Give him his due, she wasn't the only one good with their hands: so was he. He'd had their first place looking really nice, nursery and everything,

when they'd had to move to make room for the twins she'd
been as shocked as him to find out from the hospital she was
expecting. He'd kind of lost interest then, but he could still
put up shelves and fix dimmer switches and hang doors the
other way round, if she nagged him right; and he'd been as
upset as her; she knew he had, even if he'd pretended not,
having to leave when they couldn't keep up with the
mortgage, being jammed in a hostel for the homeless with a
load of people they didn't know, and wouldn't want to if
they'd had the choice. He'd gone on the dole and hated it,
and then picked up odds and ends of work she'd sometimes
rather not have known about until, leafing through the free
weekly newspaper—no more buying the local rag, and she
couldn't always get to the library to read it for nothing—
she'd spotted the ad for a groundsman/janitor at St. Catherine's School. House provided.

It had seemed like the answer to prayer. She'd pinched
herself to stay awake until Craig got back from wherever
he'd gone—drowning his sorrows, if she knew him—and
done her best not to shout at him for getting home so late,
and showed him the advert before he could drag her off to
bed. He'd said a bloke with his skills ought to have better
than doing a caretaker's job for a load of giggling, stuck-up
girls in swank uniforms, but anything to keep her quiet and
he'd phone tomorrow to see what was what. . . .

And, whatever it was, he'd got it. And she'd made him
get it. She had nobody to blame for herself that he'd come
round to seemingly enjoying the job. His own boss, near as
made no difference, provided the work got done; and
because he was good at it, it did. Set his own hours, only
emergencies to spoil the routine, indoors when it rained, out
in the sunshine when it was fine . . .

"Bleeding sight too fine, the last few weeks." Julie,
resolutely deaf to the sounds of combat from the lounge, sat
at her kitchen table, smoking. The kitchen windows—
small, high, with leaded panes—were wide open. This was
not to let out the smell of tobacco, but rather to let in as

much of a breeze as there was. Craig had promised, for what seemed like forever, to borrow one of the electric fans from the school store (just like he'd promised to fix the broken video, plonk the kids in front of it, and give her a rest, but no, he was always too busy). And when she reminded him, he told her he'd taken the last of them into the classrooms that very day, and there were more on order, but she'd have to wait. Which she'd no way of telling whether it was true or not, but catch her and the kids sitting in that garden to get stung and bitten by wasps and all them creepy-crawlies from the spinney, and mosquitoes from the pond.

Nature Study classes! Those girls had it easy—much easier than she'd ever had, and what she couldn't tell them about the birds and bees wasn't worth knowing, but she'd bet they wouldn't believe her—or need to. Just went to show what money could do for you. She'd like to see how those toffee-nosed bitches would cope with three toddlers (maybe four) and an old-fashioned house (never mind the deputy head calling it quaint: the cow didn't have to live in it, did she?) and a husband who wasn't there most of the time, who left her to fit plugs and knock in nails and move furniture and be baked alive night and day without any sign the awful weather would change. . . .

"Baked alive—yeah! If you can call this living." Julie dragged in a last mouthful of smoke before lighting her next cigarette from the ashes of the first. She shivered, despite the heat, and looked around the little kitchen with weary eyes. There were dirty dishes on the draining board, last night's washing-up still in the rack, and a pile of mending beside the sewing machine in its chipped plastic case. "If I went and cut my bleeding throat this minute, there's nobody who'd blame me. I'd be a bleeding sight better off than I am now—at least I wouldn't be stuck in this hole with those brats and him, the bastard. . . ."

Her glance fell upon the left-hand drawer of the dresser. "Cut my throat," she said again softly. Questioningly. "Leave him with the kids . . . Take them with me?" She sat up. "And have him free to play the field before I'm cold? If he's not doing it already," she reminded herself with grim humour. "Wouldn't put it past him. Wish I'd the chance myself, but—oh, no . . ."

The cigarette fell in the ashtray as she clapped her hands to her mouth, gulped, swallowed, and rushed for the sink. She hung over the side, her head down, and retched miserably until her legs gave way and she sank, groaning, to the chilly lino floor. *Not* three kids. Four. What she wouldn't give to have her time over again. Life wasn't fair—and the most unfair bit was that the lucky ones never seemed to realise their luck. She could tell them a thing or two. How she'd love to knock the smug smiles off the faces of those conceited young bitches with their posh new clothes and la-di-da talk and their lives all mapped out for them, and money to get rid of unwanted brats, if they were daft enough to slip up, handed to them on a plate like everything else . . .

"Bitches." Julie groaned again, and her head fell back. There were tears in the eyes that gazed blankly at the ceiling. "Bitches—string myself up and you'd none of you care, no more than Craig, the bastard. . . ."

And then she rolled over on her side to be thoroughly, horribly sick.

"WHY, GOOD EVENING, Mrs. Franklin—although," the speaker added with a glance at the clock above the school's main entrance, "I could almost still say *good afternoon*, couldn't I?" She tittered. "Don't you find the heat oppressive? Would you care for a hand with all your bits and bobs? And I can save you the bother of fetching the classroom key by letting you in with my own."

"Oh, that *would* be kind, Miss Shorey." Gladys Franklin, methodically unloading cardboard boxes from the boot of her car, smiled her gratitude. "It certainly is—oppressive, I mean. Now, if I could just . . ." She consulted the sheet of paper with which she'd been fanning herself. "No, I haven't forgotten anything. . . . But do you know in all the years I've been teaching, this is the first time I've found my memory so unreliable I've needed to write everything down?"

Kathleen Shorey clicked her tongue and made sympathetic noises. Gladys suddenly realised how her words might sound to the deputy headmistress, and hurried to set her straight. "It's the heat, I'm sure of it. I won't believe it's my age!" She smiled again, a little wildly. "I can't remember when I last had a decent night's sleep, and one feels so . . . so dreadfully foggy, as it were. Out of mental focus, if you know what I mean."

Miss Shorey moved closer, and, after a quick look over her shoulder, murmured that she knew exactly what Mrs. Franklin meant. A person would have to be practically inhuman not to have found the past three weeks . . . intolerable.

In her turn, Gladys lowered her voice. "Not everyone has your tolerance, Miss Shorey. And, if you'll forgive my contradicting you, perhaps it's been . . . somewhat longer than three weeks?"

Kathleen Shorey sighed and nodded. It was clear that she was more than happy to permit the contradiction. "One rather loses track of time," she said. "In circumstances such as these . . ."

The two women exchanged glances. "Yes, inhuman," said Gladys, at last. "Unfeeling. Inconsiderate . . ."

"Inconsiderate of the views of anyone else," responded Kathleen promptly. "Opinionated; stubborn. Uncooperative." She picked up the topmost cardboard box and achieved a thin smile. "Unhelpful."

"Oh, yes." Gladys favoured the deputy head with a knowing look. "Not, of course, that anyone could ever accuse you, Miss Shorey, of being unhelpful. Indeed, if it hadn't been for you, I doubt if we would be as far advanced in our work as we are."

"*Last* term," came the waspish reminder as Gladys added

one or two more boxes to Kathleen's pile, picked up her own bigger burden, and followed the deputy head indoors. "This term, I fear, I've been of regrettably less . . . use to you—indeed, to any of the Adult Education Staff—than I've been able to be in the past."

Gladys looked wise. "Able, Miss Shorey—or allowed? One simply can't help noticing . . ."

Miss Shorey sighed and said nothing. Her silence might have been caused by the echoing of footsteps in a long, empty corridor—or it might not.

After a few moments Mrs. Franklin went on:

"Though one must say, there appear to be some people who—notice—rather too much. Or who try to."

Still Miss Shorey said nothing, though her sigh and nod were most eloquent. The pair turned a corner and went out through an external door into a covered walkway.

"I have a great dislike," said Mrs. Franklin, "of people interfering in my affairs."

"I do understand," said Miss Shorey. "Personal privacy—professional, as well—they're very important. If one is fully confident of one's ability to do one's job, it is more than impertinent for—others—to doubt that ability, Mrs. Franklin." Her cheeks were flushed: perhaps from the effort of opening another door as she held the boxes; perhaps not. "Not impertinent—no. It's—it's positively insulting!"

"Ignorance," said Glady's Franklin, "that's all it is." Striding along another long, empty corridor, she tossed her head as well as she could for the height of the piled containers in her arms. "I'm the first to admit that we—all—have our own, particular areas of . . . of expertise, and knowledge. One simply can't expect to know everything about . . . well, everything. It's just not humanly possible. . . ."

"Inhuman," Kathleen reminded her grimly as she paused beside a classroom door, balanced her burden on one plump hip, and fished the master key from her pocket.

"Inconsiderate," offered Gladys as the key turned. "*And*

insulting—I couldn't agree more." The door creaked open, and the part-time teacher smiled her thanks to the permanent member of staff, standing well back to allow Miss Shorey to precede her. "Who could possibly approve of—of unwarranted interference in one's work?"

"Nobody with any pride in themselves or their achievements—in theory, that is." Kathleen deposited her boxes on the big oblong bench with its grid-marked surface, then turned to assist Gladys in her own unloading. "But theory, I'm afraid, must sometimes be very different from practice, Mrs. Franklin. Circumstances alter cases." She tapped the top of the bench with a deliberate finger. "One has, if you'll pardon the pun, to cut one's coat according to one's cloth. . . ."

Obligingly, Gladys chuckled. "To take's one's medicine," she suggested, starting to empty her first box as Kathleen moved away from the needlework department's cutting-out table towards the window side of the room. "To grin and bear it . . ."

Miss Shorey did not respond, except with a faint sigh; which might have been coincidence. "To suffer in silence?" Experimentally Gladys clashed the blades of her scissors together. "To bite the bullet—my goodness, that sounds bloodthirsty!" She stabbed bead-headed pins in and out of her strawberry pincushion. "Of course, one would never advocate violence as any sort of solution. . . ."

Against the weathered brick of a building still, after forty years, carelessly referred to by members of the school as new, tangled branches of thicket and bush and flowering shrub pressed close. Kathleen Shorey, gazing in silence from the window, watched bees busying themselves among the gaudy blossoms, diving time upon time into the depths after gold, tireless in their devotion, clambering out at last to fly with their treasure back to the hive where their efforts would, with no need of prompting, be recognised as having been for the good of all. Should danger threaten (rogue robber bees, hornets) the bees would defend themselves—

their hive—their queen. They were prepared to fight; to sting; to kill. Interlopers were not permitted to live. There could be only one queen in the hive. . . .

"Good evening, Mrs. Franklin." A pause. "Miss Shorey."

Both women jumped as that infuriating voice addressed them from the open classroom door.

Three

I T WAS ALL the more infuriating (Kathleen couldn't help but reflect) that Miss Thoday seemed so utterly unaware of just how . . . infuriating she was. Her presence—her very person—was casting an ever more virulent blight upon the life of one who had been, before the recent changes at St. Catherine's School, a contented soul; and Miss Avis Thoday just didn't *care*.

Perhaps Kathleen, on the other hand, cared too much? Had her caring affected her sense of proportion, her judgement? It was hard, in the circumstances, to be impersonal, but . . .

Miss Thoday was tall, slim, stately. Kathleen Shorey was . . . none of these. In fairness, she could hardly blame Avis for her own lack of stature, elegance, authority. . . .

But she could—yes, and did—deplore the apparently heedless—heartless—way in which the new head had made her unhappy deputy *care* about the fact that she was short, plump, and pepper-and-salt instead of crisp, dignified grey. Her stoutness and untinted hair had never in the past troubled Kathleen Shorey; they should not have troubled her now: but they did. For the first time in her life she found herself hovering in front of beauty counters in local pharmacies, reading the labels on boxes of dye, on packets of diet food. Only the knowledge that Allingham was a town where it was almost impossible to keep a secret held her back from committing herself to purchases so uncharacteristic that every pupil in the school would be sniggering, she feared, before nightfall . . . and she writhed at this fear, and moved away. And brooded as she went.

Even at weekends she could not stop brooding. Was the school already sniggering? Did the girls sneer as they made comparisons between the brisk, modern super-efficiency of Avis Thoday, M.A., and—Kathleen winced—the more easygoing, old-fashioned rule that she herself, a mere Bachelor of Arts, had continued from the days of dear Miss Waide? She had seen no real need for change after the sad retirement of her—of Miss Thoday's—predecessor. . . . Perhaps she should have done. Perhaps she—

But it was too late. The appointment had been made, had been ratified by the board of governors; Avis Thoday was now the headmistress of St. Catherine's School—and there was nothing to be done about it.

Nothing at all . . .

ON TUESDAY MORNING, Kathleen entered the school with a spring in her step and a smile on her lips. Despite the continuing oppression of the weather, she had slept well the previous night. Her slumber had been broken by only pleasant dreams, for, throughout Monday, she had managed to avoid everything but the briefest courtesies of professional intercourse between herself and her superior. A summons to Miss Thoday's study had been thwarted by a—legitimate—plea of exams to invigilate, papers to mark, anxious pupils and (not only after hours) parents to placate. The end of term drew ever nearer. St. Catherine's girls—Katies—were being forced at last to acknowledge the imminent approach of the real world; and Kathleen Shorey, who had always felt a close affinity with "her" namesake children, was determined to encourage and support them to the last.

Nodding pleasantly to the handful of girls who had come in early for special coaching, she made her way to the main notice board. Among the myriad lists of tennis and swim-

ming teams, fixture dates, certificates won, and tests still to
be taken, the school's master timetable was pinned for all to
see. She must refresh her memory about which public
examinations were to take place, and when: invigilating was
a task most of her colleagues were only too pleased to
relinquish, if the chance presented itself, as she would make
sure that it did. She must check the class hours of young
Claire Summers, who had been showing signs of rebellion
and a swollen head since her success in last term's school
play, and whose parents had asked that Miss Shorey might
have a long talk with the girl. She must—

She must get away without being seen.

Did the woman never rest? Was she never off duty? Did
she never forget her position, her responsibilities? Avis
Thoday—with not a hair out of place, the fullness of her
academic gown draped (at this hour!) neatly from her
shoulders—was standing in front of the notice board,
engaged in conversation with the janitor. Was she trying to
teach young Garner his business? He looked as happy to be
talking—listening—to the headmistress as deputy Shorey,
at this or any hour, could be . . .

Some silent, empathetic vibration tweaked an invisible
string between Kathleen Dorothea Shorey, B.A. (Hons.),
and Craig Andrew Garner, failed apprentice electrician,
general handyman (unqualified). He raised his head; he
glanced in her direction; he brightened. A gleam appeared in
his eyes, and he ventured a grin. There was no doubt he was
a good-looking rascal. Kathleen was almost tempted to grin
back, but restrained herself as she tried to reverse unobtru-
sively along the corridor down which she had hurried with
such high hopes not a minute before.

Too late. "Ah. Miss Shorey." Miss Thoday dismissed Mr.
Garner with a quick nod. He grimaced, thrust his hands in
his pockets, and walked off, breaking into a jaunty whistle
once a few yards safely separated him from the headmistress.

Avis watched him depart with a pucker between brows

whose fine arch owed nothing—Kathleen had to concede—to tweezers. Much against her inclination, she found
herself being drawn remorselessly into the orbit of Avis
Thoday even before the new headmistress recollected herself to turn upon her deputy that cool, grey, calculating
gaze—rather less cool than on other occasions, perhaps—
that had followed Craig Garner out of sight.

"Good morning, Miss Shorey." A punctilious—forced?—
smile of greeting. Kathleen, likewise, must force a smile in
reply. Miss Thoday's cheeks were slightly flushed; her voice
sounded a little harsh in Kathleen's ears. "Another busy day,
no doubt?"

"That," said Miss Shorey, "is what I was on the point of
checking." She dragged her gaze from Miss Thoday's
face—it sometimes seemed that the woman possessed a
near-hypnotic quality—and focused it firmly on the notice
board behind. "There are indeed, as I recall, a great many
matters that I expect to take up a good deal of my time
during the day—so many that I'm not able to say, without
checking, what they are. If you will excuse me—"

Avis took a deep breath and raised a pale, manicured
hand. "So busy, so early? Ten past eight," she reminded her
deputy, with a speaking glance at the expensive watch on
her wrist. She contrived another smile. "Suppose that, once
you have checked . . . whatever it is that makes so many
demands on your valuable time, you could spare me, let us
say, just half an hour in my office?"

Now her smile was less forced: Kathleen suspected she
was taking a perverse pleasure in the exchange. "Fifteen
minutes owed from yesterday," said Miss Thoday. "Fifteen
for today, and time afterwards to powder your nose before
Assembly at twenty to nine." The grey eyes tried to twinkle
at a joke, poorly shared. "And then, who knows? If we can
squeeze in one more quarter of an hour before you go home
this evening, you'll actually be in credit for tomorrow,
won't you?"

Kathleen Shorey found it easier to agree than to argue.

For one fleeting moment, she had wondered if Avis Thoday might have displayed a weakness: from the way the woman rode roughshod (but with undoubted politeness) over the opinions of others, she must accept that she had not. The iron hand in the velvet glove: the mask of courtesy hiding the face of . . . of megalomania? Whatever it hid, there was—as she had said last week to Mrs. Franklin—something inhuman about Miss Avie Thoday. . . .

THE POSTMAN SLIPPED a small bundle of envelopes through Lois Tanner's letter box just after eight o'clock on Wednesday morning. He was about to make his way back down the path to his waiting pushbike when he noticed that her pint of semiskimmed milk still stood sentinel on the doorstep.

Too young for a heart attack, even with all the upset she'd been having lately; not the kind to have gone away without cancelling, especially midweek, and with a business to run, the whole town knew she couldn't spare the time to leave. Especially now.

"Been up half the night worrying, I shouldn't wonder, poor cow." And Postman Pat drummed a kindly tattoo on the knocker, in case Ms. Tanner had overslept.

She had. Like so many others that long, hot summer, Lois wasn't sleeping very well; but she was sleeping worse than most—as most of Allingham knew. The rattle of the postman's knock reverberated harshly into already discordant dreams and brought her, heavy-eyed, struggling up from the exhausted depths of slumber, to face another difficult day.

Difficult? The understatement of the year. Lois groaned as she stumbled along to the bathroom and splashed cold water on a face whose muscles of jaw and cheek and brow were stiff with overnight tension. The dentist had warned that she was grinding her teeth in her sleep: had made a splint of heavy-duty moulded plastic which she'd twice bitten clean through. Now he'd told her she must wait until the new metal appliance arrived from the laboratory. Which would take ten days, at least. . . .

Ten days. A lot could happen in ten days. A lot could happen, if it came to that, in far fewer than ten: Lois felt her mouth curl sideways in a wry smile as she contemplated recent events. Ten days ago, Ms. Lois had been Mrs. Nicholas Tanner, joint owner with her best friend, Marianne Carmel Gordon, of Stitcherie, the discreetly expensive needlecraft and handiwork shop on one of the best sites in Allingham's High Street. . . .

She had tried for months to ignore her suspicions: tried to suppress instinctive, emotional fears that logic—based on the trust of a long friendship, on twenty years of marriage—insisted could not exist. Emotion and logic made a tumultuous subliminal mix. Why else would she have begun that war of unconscious attrition against her own body? Nick working late; Marianne—so close a friend that they'd often been taken for sisters—forever disappearing on buying trips for which she had remarkably little to show; phone calls that somehow changed in tone when she entered the room in response to her partner's summons. . . .

Either partner; either room. Husband or colleague, she had been close to them both—legally tied to them both; had shared telephone, chequebook, solicitor . . .

Solicitor.

He couldn't. She couldn't. Surely. In so short a time as this . . . to have decided in such detail what they wanted from her; to have taken the first steps towards achieving it? He or she, the instigator? Who was being egged on by whom? Not he, not she alone, but *they*. They must have been planning it, behind her back, for weeks. . . .

Lois, stiffening her spine over her cup of coffee, read the letter again. Marianne—"our client, Mrs. Gordon"—wished, in view of her imminent departure from the Allingham area—*behind her back, for weeks*—to give formal notice of her intention to dissolve the partnership in the business known as Stitcherie. In accordance with their original agreement, she was hereby offering Mrs. Tanner the chance to buy her out before she attempted to dispose of her share in the business elsewhere. Acting on her instructions, Messrs. Carr & Bury, Solicitors and Commissioners for Oaths, would be pleased to discuss suitable terms, and would be grateful if she would advise when it would be convenient. . . .

"Suitable terms." Lois allowed the letter to slip from her fingers to the table. In her pale face her eyes lost their immediate focus as she looked back into the past, and frowned. Suitable terms. Money. Payment due . . .

She shook herself back to the present, although part of her mind still brooded on matters monetary. The typist at Messrs. Carr & Bury had evidently had a busy time of it—typists, plural? Did one woman smirk, or did several giggle together, at the curious coincidence of having two such spiteful letters to send to the same woman on the same day? No, *spiteful* suggested a personal element, and as far as Lois knew, she had never met anyone from Carr & Bury in her life; had never even—her mouth curled again—seen anyone, either. As far as she knew.

The spite wasn't coming from the black symbols on the paper, or from the fingers that had placed them there; it was coming from . . . *Them.* Nick and Marianne; Marianne and Nick—who was hereby giving notice of his wish to enter into a formal separation arrangement from his wife, Lois Adelaide Tanner, with a view to pursuing a dissolution of the marriage after the statutory period . . .

"Men," announced Lois Adelaide Tanner to an empty room, "are absolute bastards. Without exception." Her eyes grew harsh and unforgiving as she did further calculations in her head. "Why women are fool enough to let themselves be exploited, I'll never know—but *I've* no intention of playing the fool. Any man who thinks I'm going to let him get away with anything—*anything*—he does that he shouldn't be doing . . . he'd damn well better think again!"

She glanced at the clock and pushed the rest of her letters, unopened, in a heap to the side of her coffee cup. Time to be off to the shop. Bills and business correspondence always went straight there: nothing here looked as if it was of importance. Nothing that couldn't wait until later, until tomorrow. She'd be too tired to bother with circulars and junk mail when she reached home this evening after work . . . long after. She did not plan to waste time coming back here when she could be preparing to stake her undoubted claim . . .

"I've learned my lesson," muttered Lois, gathering folds of pastel satin in a careful cotton embrace, "after last week." Once more, the wry twist of the mouth. "Lesson . . . Ha! Nobody catches me the same way twice!"

And the glint in the eye of Lois Adelaide Tanner boded ill for anyone who might cross her path in the future.

Four

As THE HEAT waved had endured, so had England. Baked daily ever more dry beneath a relentless sun, slowly stifling under a thickening haze of photochemical smog, there was not the tiniest corner of the country across which, even for an instant, blew during those insufferable, interminable days one merciful breath of air.

A curvaceous Allingham housewife accepted the afternoon invitation of her next-door neighbour—a bachelor—to try out her new bikini in the privacy of his swimming pool. The trial proved rather more private than her husband, on his return from work, felt able to approve. Hearing laughter from the other side of the hedge, he had ascertained the cause with a tiptoe movement that went unobserved through the inability of the pair by the pool to pay attention to anything or anyone but their own immediate affairs . . . and, following a further tiptoe movement to the shed at the bottom of his garden, he had taken a short—and literal—cut to his neighbour's garden through the territorial greenery, in defence of his masculine honour and the sanctity of his marital hearth.

The ensuing imbroglio eventually ended with the bachelor in Intensive Care, the blonde in the mortuary, the hedge-cutter husband cooling his heels in the cells of Allingham police station, and Trewley and Stone, at the end of a hectic day, in their office, putting the finishing touches to preliminary statements and lamenting the heat-enhanced frailties of the whole human race.

"Manslaughter," Trewley said, "or I'm a Dutchman, that's how he'll plead." He stuffed his handkerchief back in his pocket after mopping his face and neck for the umpteenth time. Even at top speed, the pilfered electric fan couldn't be expected to perform miracles. "Reckon I could almost go along with that, in a way. Not agreeing to murder, I mean, the way the weather's driven everyone crazy . . ."

Stone's head came up from the papers she was studying. She narrowed her eyes at her superior and took a deep, controlled breath. "Are you seriously suggesting that a man is entitled to—to chop his wife into mincemeat, and then have the cheek to expect a lighter sentence, simply because he gets a bit hot under the collar one afternoon? Why, that's about the most—"

"*In a way*, I said! Smooth your blasted bristles, girl, and credit me with as much respect for the victim—male, female, bug-eyed monster from Mars—as the next man! Or," he added, "woman." The bulldog ventured a grin as Stone's furious expression began to soften. "All right?"

"Uh—right." A little sheepishly, she returned the grin. "Sorry, sir. Blame the heat: *crazy* isn't the word. We're all starting to get things out of proportion." She glanced up at the fan on top of the filing cabinet. "Have you, um, noticed how even Sergeant Pleate has been making odd remarks over the past few days?"

Trewley volunteered his forthright opinion of Sergeant Pleate, then sighed and leaned back in his chair. "It's late. It's hot. I'm tired—and don't try to tell me you aren't, because I won't believe you." Stone didn't try. Trewley fumbled again for his handkechief. "We've had a hell of a time of it this week—these past few weeks. I should think we've just about seen the lot. Why the devil can't folk realise it only makes things worse if they drink too much?"

"Alcohol," appended the doctor manqué, in the interests of scientific accuracy, as her colleague mopped his brow.

"Too much alcohol—quite apart from the damage it does to your liver—will dehydrate you and make you feel ghastly whether it's the height of summer, or the middle of winter. That's why, in a perfect world, sensible drinkers would drink measure-for-measure booze and fruit juice, if they don't care for water. Only it isn't, of course, and they never do."

Trewley had closed his eyes. His voice, as he spoke, was weary. "If everyone used their common sense, Stone, you and I'd be out of a job, because it *would* be pretty damn near a perfect world. Common sense doesn't mix too well with crime."

Stone, whose youthful idealism had not been entirely extinguished by her years under Trewley's command, ignored this melancholy reflection to press on with her lecture. "On the other hand, it's quite difficult to drink too much water, though it's not altogether unknown. As a general rule, the more nonalcoholic liquid you can pour into yourself, the better—but there've been several cases where people have actually overdosed themselves to death on water. For exam—"

The brown bloodhound eyes opened in reproach. "This is no time for nonsense, girl. Let's get off home before—"

"Cross my heart! Somebody swallowed bleach by mistake and phoned the hospital the minute she realised what she'd done, and they told her to drink plenty of water, so she did. And . . ." The former medic hesitated in her discourse to the layman. "And it, um, diluted her insides, including her central nervous system, which meant the electric impulses couldn't reach her brain. And the poor woman, um, stopped working. And died."

"I'll stick to beer," said Trewley, after a pause.

"I once read of a man," returned Stone brightly, "who decided to fill himself up with something else when he was told to cut down on the beer. His liver must have been like leather, because he filled himself up with *three gallons* of water a day—which waterlogged his brain, so that he passed out. And while he was unconscious he vomited, and choked on it. So his lungs were irreparably damaged, and—"

"Stone!"

"Sorry, sir. But you did ask." She subdued the twinkle in her eye as she tried to stand on her dignity. "Or at the very least, you cast nasturtiums on my integrity, and—"

And the telephone rang on Trewley's desk, making both of them jump.

"Trewley," barked the bloodhound, welcoming the interruption even if, as he suspected, it was one that would set him off once more on a criminous trail. "Yes?"

After fifteen seconds' intense listening, he shuddered as he signalled for Stone to pick up the extension, and began groping among the clutter of papers on his own desk for pencil and paper. "Hang on . . . Right." His face registered an unease his sergeant had seldom noticed before, and his voice was grim. "Let's have it again, can we?"

"St. Catherine's School," came the metallic tones of PC Benson along the telephone wire. "The bit they call the new building—the red brick, not the swank stone facing. About half an hour ago, at the start of the evening class in needlework, this woman was at her sewing machine, and it—well, sir, it electrocuted her."

"Electric impulses *could* reach the brain," Trewley found himself muttering.

"Sorry, sir?"

"Never mind me." Trewley glared at Stone, though it was hardly her fault that, for one wild moment, he'd been tempted to ask if the woman in question had been drinking water. "Carry on, Benson. Uh . . . dead?"

"Oh, yes, sir, they phoned for an ambulance straight off, and the medical people say there was nothing to be done. Hardly surprising, really. I've rung for Doc Watson: he's on his way. I've chivvied all the needleworkers off to join the cookery people, sir, and told 'em to see they have cups of tea and stuff until we can deal with 'em. Some of those females are in a pretty bad way with shock."

Stone snorted wrathfully but didn't speak. Benson said at once: "Sorry, Sarge. But the one bloke there was about the only person who kept his head—Boy Scouts, be prepared and that. Seems he grabbed a length of material and sort of lassoed her with it to pull her away from the contact, then told his wife to try heart massage—she's a first-aider— while he switched it off at the wall with his walking stick. It's wooden with a rubber tip, you see."

"Highly commendable," growled Trewley as Stone nodded her approval of this action. "What about you?"

"I got there ten minutes or so after it happened, sir. Everyone was naturally in a bit of a state by then, so, like I said, I sent 'em off to join the cookery class and asked 'em to sit tight. I locked the classroom door, and the key's in my pocket right now."

"And where are you? In the car?"

A note of constraint entered the normally cheerful tones of Constable Benson. "Headmistress's office, sir. Miss Thoday. They had to use her phone for the three-nines call, and she went back with whoever it was to . . . keep an eye on things, she said." The slight pause that here ensued might have suggested to an alert listener that PC Benson had glanced over his shoulder before continuing his report. "She, er, volunteered to stay on guard in the classroom until you got here, sir. Very keen to do her bit, she was." A further pause; an embarrassed confession. "Tell the truth, sir, I had a spot of bother getting her to join the others in the cookery room."

"Umph." Trewley's three teenage daughters had friends who attended St. Catherine's. Like teenagers everywhere, they gossiped. He offered no further comment, critical or otherwise, on Benson's behaviour. "So what's your reading of the situation? Suspicious death—or plain accident?"

"Dunno, sir. I mean, it's hard to tell. Electricity can be dangerous, right enough, but . . . a sewing machine? Do they often fuse—or whatever this's done—and . . . well, and kill people?"

Once more Stone observed that uneasy expression on the superintendent's face. "You said it yourself, lad, electricity can be dangerous, though I agree you don't normally expect to risk life and limb when you're hemming a sheet. Still, the sergeant and I will talk it over together while we're on our way to you. Quite an expert, she is."

Stone gasped, but was far too conscious of the need to maintain on-air discipline to voice any objection to this outrageous remark until Trewley had ordered Benson back on duty, and broken the connection. "For heaven's sake—sir—has the hot weather finally got to you? Fancy saying I'm an expert!"

A forced bulldog rumble, deep in Trewley's throat, might almost have been a laugh. "Did I say what sort? A black belt in judo, now. If that's not expert, I'd like to know what is. Besides," he added as she choked, "a nice, peaceful technical discussion on the road'll help take my mind off your driving, won't it, Sergeant?"

"So it will, sir." And Stone strode out of the office at a pace she knew her heavyweight superior would never be able to maintain for long.

Once they were buckled into their seat belts, Trewley settled back with a sigh, opening the passenger window as far as it would go, letting the breeze play across his heated brow. "They don't, do they?"

The sergeant was accustomed to the sometimes elliptical thought processes of her colleague. "With all due respect, sir, why ask me? I can only just about sew on a button." A pause, which some might have thought pointed. "If you recall." Last week's mangled-tie-and-collar-button episode had been followed by some crisp comment and, eventually, some competent—if decidedly uninspired—stitchery on the part of the female half on the team, after a frantic appeal from one who had realised that his wife would have Something To Say if he went home with his clothing in tatters. "You know I'm no needlewoman. I can't tell you anything about sewing machines, except that they're supposed to save time and trouble."

She chuckled. "In theory. Speaking personally, in practice they don't. I was always bottom of my domestic science classes for as long as we had them. I couldn't even pin and tack straight, never mind sew a decent seam. . . ." She remembered her companion's routine complaint about her driving skill and her enthusiasm for the accelerator, and added casually, "I was always worried the machine might run away with me—which it generally did. I never could seem to gauge the right amount of pressure for the foot pedal. Odd, that."

"Explains a lot." Trewley glanced sideways and watched her lip quiver. "Now, be serious, girl. *Is* it possible, do you reckon?"

She didn't pretend not to know what he meant. "To hocus a plug to electrocute whoever uses the machine when they switch it on? Come off it, sir, you must know as much as I do about fitting plugs, if not more. Few people don't, nowadays, when it's so easy."

Trewley scowled. "Red wire for live, black for neutral, green for earth. That's how it was when I was a boy, and I haven't been happy with the new system since it came in—and there's no need to remind me that's more than twenty years, because I know. But I still can't seem to get along with it, though I've never worked out why. . . ."

"There's no obvious logic to the system, that's why." Stone frowned as she changed physical gear to slow the car into a bend, and mental gear as she pondered the domestic electricity supply. "Brown for live, when you'd logically expect brown to be earth; blue for neutral, when you'd expect neutral to be neither one thing nor the other; and yellow-green striped, neither one thing nor the other, for earth. None of which makes much sense, at first sight—but it does actually serve a purpose, sir." Once more, the medical mind was unable to resist enlightening another, less informed. "For people who are colour blind—"

"Colour blind? Not if they're keen on sewing, surely."

"More men than women are colour blind," began Stone, and then paused. "Benson told us there was only one man in the class. . . . Poor St. Catherine's." She was not a Katie, but nobody in Allshire could be unaware of the importance of the school in the local—if not national—education system. "After the year they've had," mused Detective Sergeant Stone out loud, "this could just about finish them. . . ."

And Detective Superintendent Trewley did not disagree.

Five

"THE LAST THING they need." Trewley grunted, ruthlessly brushing aside a stray insect that had flown in through the open window. "Their name was pretty well mud in certain quarters to begin with, but now they've started bumping one another off—*if* they have, and it's not just an accident. . . ."

"Either way," said Stone, "I wouldn't give much for the chances of next year's intake holding at this year's level. After all, mud, um, sticks. The fact that whatever's happened happened to somebody in the evening class, not to one of the—the regular pupils, won't make a blind bit of difference. Nervous parents aren't going to want"—she gave a lively impression of an upper-class matron—"their gels runnin' any risks, what?"

Trewley, thinking of his three nubile daughters, sighed: there were risks, and risks. He rubbed his chin and scowled at passing shop windows. "Of course, if anyone really did want to—to make some blasted statement about all that carry-on, I'd've expected more of a . . . another picket round the theatre, or a protest march along the blasted footpath. Not creeping about the place twiddling bits of wire together, or whatever they did. If they did. Damn it, Stone, all that was two terms ago!"

"They say revenge doesn't spoil with keeping, sir." She shook her dark head slowly as she pondered the problem. "I have to agree, though, in this case it seems unlikely. Who in their right mind, six months after the event, is going to feel so worked up over a rerouted footpath and a planning application that—?"

Her companion's snort prevented completion of her rhetorical question. "In their right mind, you said? Use your brains, girl. Is there anyone in this benighted town—in the whole county—in the *county*, for heaven's sake—who's been *in their right mind* since this damned heat wave began? What was that you said earlier about getting things out of proportion? Some of those conservationists can be moody blighters at the best of times—which, when they've lost a public enquiry, it isn't."

"Wasn't, sir," she ventured to correct him. "Be fair. The new theatre is a fait accompli: they had their first production there at the end of last term, remember? It was reviewed in the *Argus. Othello*."

"Another jealous husband," muttered Trewley, who had, pleading pressure of work, been able to escape the play, but who'd been forced to hear about it in exhaustive detail from his proud neighbour, whose daughter had shared the role of Cassio with a girl who had begun by being her closest friend—and who was now, envy at her greater success having soured their relationship, her sworn foe. "Jealousy's a terrible thing, Stone. You and young What's-His-Name don't know how lucky you are."

Stone didn't risk correcting him again. Once per conversation was as often as she cared to risk until the temperature had returned to normal. "Anyway, sir, if you recall . . . on the first night, there were people with banners hanging around outside, but almost nobody bothered showing up for any of the other performances. And the footpath walkers do seem to have accepted the diversion, after a bit of grumbling. Miss . . . Shorey, is it? The acting head. She was forever on the phone last term, complaining about trespass, but since the new head arrived, we haven't heard a peep."

Trewley rumbled with lazy mirth at her side. "You can't really blame Benson for being scared of the woman. By all accounts she's a pretty tough cookie. If," he added, risking a joke, "you'll pardon my sexist choice of words."

But Stone was slowing the car for the St. Catherine's turn and did not deign to reply.

PC Benson was waiting for them at the main entrance and led the way quickly along the corridors to a door outside which the stolid, shining buttons of PC Hedges now stood guard in place of his more loquacious and volatile friend.

Inside the sewing room the statutory bustle attendant upon any sudden death was at its height. Trewley greeted the silent sentry with a swift nod, poked his head around the door, surveyed the scene, and withdrew a few paces to confer with Dr. Watson. Without that much-bearded medico's official endorsement of the corpse as a corpse, no investigation was by law allowed to proceed.

"As a doornail," Dr. Watson cheerily replied in response to the superintendent's enquiry. "Instantaneous. Wouldn't have had a clue what hit her."

"And you have?" Trewley found himself rubbing his chin. He muttered something colourful and thrust his hands deep in his trouser pockets. The golden rule of detection was that nothing must be touched until everything had been seen. Stone, he was glad to observe—though he would have expected no less—had hooked her thumbs firmly over her belt as she stood in the open doorway, and was making no attempt to intrude on the activity within.

"Two hundred and forty volts. Enough to kill anyone if the current keeps on flowing, which in this case it did. Her foot on the pedal, her hand on the metal plate as she held the sewing steady: the perfect circuit. Earthed her nicely—and did for her at the same time, poor woman."

Trewley, relieved that here—for once—was a cause of death he could understand without effort, was about to thank him for his assistance when the bright-eyed doctor pounced. "As to *exactly* how she died, you'll have to wait until I've done the postmortem. Say, a couple of hours?"

The superintendent stared. "You said—"

"You asked if I knew what hit her. I told you I did: the full force of our domestic electricity supply. But how and where it hit—apart from the entry and exit burns, which are obvious—I really wouldn't care to venture an opinion. Ask the good sergeant," he added as he gathered up his belongings and prepared to depart.

Stone, hearing herself taken in vain, looked round from the door. "Your boss wants chapter and verse on electrocution, Sergeant, and I have to make tracks for the morgue. Do me a favour—one sawbones to another—and fill him in, will you?"

"That man!" Trewley glowered at Dr. Watson as he bustled merrily mortuarywards. "How and why and where, indeed . . ."

Even the unemotional Hedges could not prevent a grin as Stone dragged her superior out of earshot so that he could air his grievances in private. "You know he only does it to wind you up, sir," she muttered. "Don't take any notice. Think of your blood pressure!"

"Blood be damned. There wasn't any, that I could see: and you?" Wordlessly she shook her head. They both knew that bloodstained bodies and studied contemplation of crime scenes did not, for Detective Sergeant Stone, sit easily together. Had there been the least sign of butchery, carnage, or gore visible from her observation post, she would, until summoned by Trewley, have found something else useful with which to occupy herself, safely out of sight.

"Well, then. Let's have it—but in English, mind. If I can't spell it, I don't want to hear it."

She had been dredging her memory even as she watched the forensic and photographic experts prosecuting their official duties, and now took a deep breath. "Doc Watson was right to be cautious about how it killed her, sir, even if the way he put it was, um, a bit . . ."

"Thank you. We'll skip that part."

"Yes, sir." She cleared her throat. "A person who dies

from being electrocuted suffers a virtually instant shock, resulting in, um, a total shutdown of the central nervous system. There's no question about that . . . but *how* it shuts down depends on whether the current goes first through the heart or through the brain. You have the choice of massive fibrillation of the heart—the muscles go into spasm—or acute paralysis of the respiratory centre of the brain, if it goes through the medulla oblongata. Which," she enlarged hastily, as a dangerous gleam appeared in her pupil's eye, "is the bit at the bottom of the brain, where it narrows—elongates—into the spinal cord."

"Umph." A thoughtful pause. "Nasty." With an effort he brightened. "People don't always die, though, do they? An uncle of mine was blown clean across the room when he was messing about with his electrics, and he survived. Why?"

"Luck," said Stone firmly. "He must have been better insulated than our friend there," she added with a quick nod towards the needlework room. "Rubber soles to his shoes, say, or a wooden handle to the screwdriver, or whatever it was he was messing about with. . . . Do you know if he suffered any aftereffects?"

"Went to bed for a week with a thumping headache, as I recall." Trewley grimaced. "I was a kid at the time, but it made a big impression. Made me think twice about tackling home electrics, believe me."

"And at work." But Stone was not cruel by nature. As Trewley never teased her for her dislike of gore, and of thunderstorms, so she would ignore in future all reference to this hitherto unsuspected weakness of her red-faced superior. "Nasty indeed, sir. Your uncle was luckier than he knew. He was probably saved by the fact that he would have been mentally and physically half-prepared for a shock: people have been killed by a far lower current, if it's unexpected. But there could have been all sorts of horrid developments later on, quite apart from some very unpleasant necrosis of the skin at the time. Gangrene—secondary haemorrhage—even an increased risk of some degenerative disease of the central nervous system, such as multiple sclerosis—compared to any of those, I'd think a few days' cerebral irritation would be a doddle."

Trewley shuddered. "If you say so." He scowled. "Are we going to be kept hanging around out here forever? What's holding everybody up?"

He raised his voice as he spoke the final words. Benson promptly materialised from around a corner, but was ignored as an answering cry came from the needlework room to the effect that another five minutes or so should see them done.

"We'll take a good look while we're waiting," decreed Trewley, his hands once more in his pockets. He strode across to the door, and Hedges moved hurriedly aside, missing Benson's foot by less than an inch. "*You've* had a good look already, Stone. Your verdict?"

"From here," she ventured, "it seems rather a pity she didn't live to finish it. Whatever it is. Not really my sort of colour scheme, but certainly eye-catching."

"It looks . . . expensive," said Trewley. "Killed for her money, maybe? If she was, of course."

Stone ventured to shake her head. "I told you, sir, I'm not much of a one for sewing . . . but I would have thought anyone with enough money to be worth being killed for would, um, rather pay someone else—an expert seamstress—to do the sewing for her. Especially when, as you say, it's such expensive material. She's used what looks like yards of satin, and that doesn't come cheap. Just think if she made a mistake and had to unpick it. The needle holes would ruin the surface—she'd be bound to snag the threads—and the point of the stitch ripper would spike more little holes all over the place. Those plain colours would show every single mark." Her voice rang with the bitter memories of youth. "The whole design could be ruined. . . ."

"Unless," suggested Trewley, hiding a grin as his ser-

geant turned pink at having betrayed such a feminine
interest in fabric, "the expert seamstress was the one who
paid for the stuff. Was *her*," he said, jerking his head
towards the plump, silent, black-haired figure that was the
still centre of a professionally bustling world. "Not everyone who goes to needlework classes has been . . . con-
scripted." The choice of word seemed to please him. "Like
you were—or my three, come to that. Some girls—
women," he amended as Stone recovered herself to frown,
"actually enjoy sewing. It's not just the . . . challenge,
they tell me. Some of 'em seriously think it's *fun*. They . . ."
His hand described a bewildered gesture in midair; then he
remembered his trouser pockets, and scowled. "They take
exams, and so on. They *pass* exams. They get qualifications! Why shouldn't our party here be one of *them*?"

A helpful cough came from his other side. "Er—she is,
sir," said PC Benson. "Leastways, I think she must be. An
expert, I mean—because of everything supposed to be
made by hand, from what it says on the door, and with the
Trades Descriptions Act . . ."

"Door?" The puzzled attention of Trewley and Stone was
turned to the glass panes, wooden panels, and serviceable
hinges of the classroom portal. A neatly painted hardboard
oblong, fastened level with brass keyhole and handle on the
centre strut, clearly identified the needlework room.

"Talk sense, lad," said Trewley. "That door's not saying
anything except name, rank, and number. And as for the
Trades Descriptions Act, I—yes, Sergeant Stone?"

"On the door of the shop?" she suggested with gentle
emphasis as Benson's ears turned pink at the tips. "You
mean that place in the High Street—Stitcherie?"

Beside her, Trewley emitted an exasperated snort, then
recovered to advise PC Benson that this time it would just
about do, but in future he'd better make sure his statements
made proper sense. "Stitcherie," he muttered, while Benson
stared at his boots. He looked again over the heads of his
forensic team at the tumble of satin, in pastel and pearl and

rich, midnight shades, on which the dead woman had evidently intended to work before her demise.

"Umph. *Expensive*'s not the word. My wife has dropped in a couple of times for wedding presents, but you damned well near enough need a solid-gold credit card to cross the threshold, they tell me. Stitcherie." He rubbed his chin, and scowled. "Stitcherie . . . I've heard gossip about that place in the last few weeks, but . . ."

Stone nodded: so had she. Like Trewley, though, she was finding it elusive.

The superintendent gave up the struggle. "It'll come. Yes. Stitcherie. So our friend here's one of the owners, is she?"

"She is." It was neither Benson nor Stone who replied, but the tallest member of the forensic team, who had paused in his filming to fiddle with something in the video camera. "You're not the only one with a wife hell-bent on emptying the bank account the minute the salary cheque's gone in." He grimaced. "I was in there last week, doing my best to stop her taking out another mortgage for some daft wall hanging this woman makes for people who must think paint and paper is vulgar. Made, I mean. Couldn't forget her, the money she cost me. That's Lois Tanner."

━━━━━━ Six ━━━━━━

"AN EXPERT," SAID Trewley again; and again, brooding, he rubbed his chin. "A professional, you could say, seeing as she made the stuff for public sale. Odd." He shrugged. "Granted, nobody can know it all—but somehow you don't imagine someone like that'd need to come to evening classes, do you?"

"Perhaps she enjoyed the company, sir." Benson, blushing, ventured a sideways look at Stone. "All girls together—begging your pardon, Sarge."

The sergeant regarded him grimly. "Plus a token male, or so you said on the phone. Your friend the first-aid expert . . . remember?"

"The scouting-for-boys bloke," said Stone's superior quickly. He didn't much care for the gleam in her eye. "Yes, well, you don't imagine a man coming to needlework classes, either. . . ." The last thing he wanted was a third murder on his hands, when the husband of the blonde bikini was complicating things by pleading provocation, and as for this one, he hadn't even started to sort it out yet. . . .

"Damn! What did I just say? Murder?" Trewley clapped himself on the forehead and groaned. "That's all I need, at the end of a day like this one's been. I didn't mean it, did I? Tell me I didn't!"

Stone at once abandoned her half-hearted skirmish with Benson. "Why, certainly, sir. If it will make you happy." Of the little group in Trewley's immediate vicinity, she alone dared risk responding to his anguished plea: her role as the dutiful sidekick had over the years involved her in far more dangerous tasks than this. "You couldn't have meant it— because you never actually said anything of the kind . . . out loud. But," she added as something in her tone made him favour her with a quizzical look, "might I hazard a guess that you were thinking it? Because," she said as the bloodhound began to rumble at her side, "if you were . . . well, you're not the only one to wonder. Sewing machines are pretty safe beasts, on the whole. Unless you stitch through your fingers by mistake. . . ." That note of bitter reminiscence returned to her voice. "But even I never managed to electrocute myself, sir. Which would seem to suggest that any suspicions—"

"We're all done in here, Mr. Trewley!"

And that, for the moment, was that.

"FOR THE BUSINESS contacts, I bet."

The preliminary findings of the forensic team had been concisely reported to a fascinated audience. Sergeant Stone had shaken her head over the wickedness that could contrive the exchange of a live wire and an earth inside the floor control of an electric sewing machine; Trewley, trusting to her superior scientific knowledge for later, private explanation, had set about his own detailed examination of the needlework room. The sergeant had made pencil jottings in her notebook; Constable Benson had been sent to warn those in the cookery room that they wouldn't have long to wait.

"That's why she'll have come to the classes." Stone, herself a practical person, could approve such enterprise on the part of another. "Networking—though not," she said, grinning, "in the, um, lacemaking sense. The others would see what she could do, be impressed, and recommend her to their friends. Or she could recruit them as, um, outworkers. Some people might be a bit shy about walking into a shop to offer their handiwork for sale, having to discuss commission and that sort of thing. But in a class . . ."

"All girls together," offered Trewley, as the pair made their way along covered walks and corridors to the witnesses waiting in the main block.

"Just so, sir," said Stone, without rancour. "Everyone on an equal footing—except that I suppose some," she said with a rueful grin, "will have been rather more equal than others."

"Then," Trewley decreed, "we'll talk first to the most equal of the lot. It's the boss's job to know what's going on, after all—and I don't necessarily mean Miss Thoday." The new headmistress might have intimidated young Benson, but Benson's superior was not so spineless.

He hoped.

"Yes, sir." Stone, brooding, failed to notice the hint of uncertainty in his tone. She frowned. "But if we've guessed right about what was going on—and if she knew . . . I wonder how she liked the idea of one of her pupils touting for custom, or whatever you want to call it, in class?"

ONCE EVERYONE FOR whom she felt tutorially responsible had been safely removed from the scene of Lois Tanner's dreadful accident, Gladys Franklin decided that she could now relax: and relax she did.

Yet this was an indulgence for which she soon had cause to reproach herself, as the traditional strong, sweet tea (courtesy of the cookery class) set about lifting even the lowest spirits. After the cookers (who hadn't seen what the needlecrafters had seen) had overcome their initial shock at the sudden irruption into their midst of these flustered newcomers, they merrily embroiled themselves in an enthusiastic discussion of what had happened, what the police might be doing about it, whether it had indeed been an accident . . . and, to Mrs. Franklin's horrified dismay, Mrs. Franklin's class began joining in. Not all the censorious stares and crisp comments of Avis Thoday could silence the speculators: they were not her pupils. Over them, the headmistress had no authority.

Over them, Gladys Franklin had . . . a measure. Stern conscience seized her, stiffening her weakened spine. She had relaxed too soon: she had allowed her nerves to get the better of her, in a manner neither more nor less than self-indulgent. Feeble. She must brace herself to set an example—and at once.

She wasted no time on words. Useless to attempt any verbal breaking into the hubbub of conjecture: undignified to have to shout. Instead, she clattered her empty cup several times in its saucer, and then placed it on the table with a bang.

Slowly she shook a stern head at the faces turned automatically towards her. Even the eye of Miss Thoday failed for once to intimidate the older woman.

Gladys cleared her throat. She inhaled deeply. "Now listen, ladies—and gentlemen." She prided herself on her sense of fair play. To be *strictly* fair, it was at first sight most *un*fair to include the few males present among those she was about to chastise: but it would be rude to ignore the presence of Mr. Harvey, who had been so very helpful when poor Mrs. Tanner's machine had . . . gone wrong; and she fancied that the men would chatter quite as much as their wives, once they were somewhere they thought nobody would overhear them.

"Listen!" She clattered the saucer again: it gave her confidence. "Now, aren't we letting things get a teensy bit out of hand? The police are *always* called to any sudden death. Just because they have asked us to wait here and answer questions later doesn't mean they believe there's . . . anything wrong."

"No?" countered Deirdre Pollard, who enjoyed television detective dramas, and didn't see why she should be denied the chance to act in their true-life equivalent. "Once they find out just what our friend Tanner was like, they'll soon start to believe there is. Dozens of people must have had it in for her, one way or another. Including—"

"Including you," supplied Jean Harvey, before Deirdre could finish. Jean's husband, Alan, at her side, sighed, but did not speak.

"Including me," agreed Mrs. Pollard, unruffled. "After that wretched business last week, I'd find it hard to argue with them if they put my name on the list. The woman annoyed me, there's no denying—though as to sheer annoyance being a—a credible motive for bumping her off . . ."

"Poetic justice?" suggested Mrs. Harvey as Deirdre gave an expressive shrug.

"Really!" cried Gladys, above Mrs. Pollard's considered acceptance of the charge. "Ladies, please. I understand how shock can affect people in many different ways, but this—this tasteless joking—"

"Who's joking?" Deirdre shrugged again. "Oh, I know that to a rational mind it would just seem like a lot of daft women squabbling: but murderers aren't rational. As the police," she said grimly now, "are well aware. They say a person has to be just a bit crazy to kill—and with everyone on edge the way we've been since this awful weather began . . ."

Her words fell into an unpleasant silence. Eyes turned from the door (propped wide open by a catering-sized tin of flour) to the huge electric fans humming at either end of the room, and thence to the high-flung sash windows through which hardly the breath of a breeze could fight its way to refresh those within. Of recent weeks cookery classes at St. Catherine's had concentrated on salads and exotic chilled puddings, rather than on anything that required the ovens to be switched on.

"Awful," echoed Mrs. Franklin despite herself, waking to the realisation that she had somehow separated teacup from saucer and was using the latter to create a closely localised current of air. Recovering, she said, "Yes . . . but we simply must try to . . . to be rational, and calm, and—and to keep cool about this." Would a psychiatrist have found significance in her final choice of adjective? "To keep things in proportion. I'm sure the—the police," she said with a gulp, "will have more important . . . That is, they won't want to listen to any nonsense about—about sewing machines. . . ."

"Won't we?" came an unexpected masculine voice from the door. "I wouldn't take a bet on that myself." And through the open door, brushing PC Benson aside with a nod, strode, on cue, Superintendent Trewley, with his Stony shadow close behind.

Above the startled gasps and murmurs of surprise, the pair introduced themselves to the assembled evening scholars, who—with one exception—regarded the two detectives in an uneasy silence that seethed with mingled curiosity and alarm. The exception was Miss Avis Thoday. As Trewley concluded his introductory remarks, she rose to her feet, and from across the room her eyes met those of the superintendent on almost equal terms.

"Mr. Trewley, I am Avis Thoday. As headmistress of St. Catherine's, and as such responsible, under the board of governors, for everything that happens on these premises, I should like to express my sincere hope that you and your colleagues will soon come to a—a suitable resolution of the distressing accident that has occurred." Did her words chime faintly with the barest hint of doubt? "The reputation of this school, while resting primarily in my hands, rests also, for the immediate future, in your own. And—"

Trewley's deeper tones drowned out the conjunction, fully extinguishing whatever had been intended to follow. "And," rumbled the bulldog, "we'll take the greatest care of its reputation, I promise you. We're thorough, we are, in the Allingham police. We don't drop things." He felt Stone vibrate quietly at his side. "Umph. Believe me, we don't—in whatever sense you like."

He wouldn't push his luck, though. He'd made his point;

he nodded a swift, polite dismissal, then turned his attention to the woman who'd been speaking when he and Stone had overheard some talk about . . .

"Nonsense about sewing machines," he quoted, and gave Gladys the benefit of his full bulldog glower. "*Nonsense* makes it all sound like a bit of a joke, doesn't it? But there's not too much to laugh at when there's somebody dead, and seems it was a fault in the sewing machine that killed her." Gladys flushed; others in the room fidgeted on their chairs and looked away. "But there. These slips of the tongue can happen, I know. Shock . . ." The bulldog, tenacious and grim, had become the far less threatening bloodhound. In the years she'd known him, Stone had never quite worked out how her chief managed that idiosyncratic, disarming metamorphosis.

"And a nasty shock it must have been for you all," went on the bloodhound, pulling a chair towards himself and sitting heavily down. Stone, her notebook and pencil at the ready, moved discreetly out of direct sight. "It helps, you know, if you can talk about it instead of bottling it up—and no, I don't mean statements. There'll be time enough for all that, but let rip with your first impressions and you could save yourselves no end of nightmares later. This weather on its own's enough to give anyone sleepless nights, never mind—well, anything else."

Stone could have applauded as, with due solemnity, the superintendent mopped his brow with his polka-dot hand-kerchief, loosened the tie at his neck, ran a weary finger around his collar, and sighed. "The quicker we can get out in the fresh air again, the happier we'll all be," he observed to the room at large. "So let's be hearing about this— nonsense—last week, shall we?"

His audience suddenly remembered who he was and why he was there.

And wondered just how long he had been there before he allowed anyone to notice him.

——————— Seven ———————

THE TEACHER SHOULD arrive before the pupils. This was the creed of Gladys Franklin: and not only because there were, in the case of her needlework projects, diverse goodies to be set out before the class could begin. Each week Gladys would bring with her a selection of pattern books; samples of rare textiles, yarns, and threads; powdered chalk for hem markers; carbon paper; tracing wheels; and other similarly nonessential but helpful aids to the Company of Dorcas, novice and skilled alike. Everyone found these items of interest; and, as Gladys explained their purpose, many would buy from her, or order fresh supplies at cost-plus-ten-percent-for-her-trouble. This income was a recognised, if unofficial, perk for the tutor. Lois Tanner might look down her nose, but even she (who more than once had spoken proudly of plain speech and direct action) had never voiced any doubt or complaint out loud.

Larger or more expensive pieces of equipment remained in, and belonged to, the school. There were two full-length mirrors, several adjustable dress forms, and all things necessary for the perfect finishing of work: ironing and separate sleeve boards, tailor's cushions, the irons (steam and dry) themselves, and that finely spiked velvet board for piled fabrics that always reminded ribald first-formers of a traffic-flattened hedgehog.

There were also, of course, the sewing machines, and the attachments that came with them.

Parents and Old Girls of St. Catherine's were generous souls, and the staff were prudent to a fault. Unless it was broken beyond repair, nothing with the most remote possibility for being useful and/or educational was ever thrown away. From somebody's great-grandmother's treadle in its oak veneer cabinet (the late-twentieth-century dearth of rubber drive belts had spurred the daytime sewing mistress to surprising heights of ingenuity) to the latest computer-driven import from Japan, there was a machine to suit every taste, and every level of ability. Purists who preferred individual to mass-produced trimmings could exchange feet to ruffle and frill and flounce as the fancy took them. The less ambitious, who might want to sew basic straight-stitch seams without even a zigzag for variety, would sit happily feeding material at their own speed through the kindly jaws of a hand-powered portable which, when not in use, slept out its hard-working retirement in a carrying case of battered green plastic, mock tweed style.

It was inevitable that those who were most comfortable with one model could be less than comfortable if circumstances conspired to make them use another. In class there was always the opportunity to swap notes, compare experiences, and try a few specimen squares out of interest; but, by and large, once a student had settled to using one particular machine, it was generally understood that she (or he) would stay settled.

At the first class of the year, Lois Tanner had wanted to know which (if any) of the modern machines was equipped with a walking foot, for quilting purposes. It seemed to Gladys that her pupil hadn't so much asked as demanded: improved acquaintance with Ms. Tanner's forthright nature showed the teacher that she probably had.

Gladys frowned. "A walking foot."

A quick quirk of the lips hinted that Lois was far from impressed by her teacher's lack of knowledge. "A special attachment," she explained, sounding rather more superior than etiquette would approve, "that allows what we might call the three-layer fabric 'sandwich' to feed through without crushing the wadding in the middle."

As several bystanders looked suitably baffled by this remark, Mrs. Franklin's frown turned to a glint-eyed look of pure annoyance. Hurriedly, for the sake of professional detachment, she suppressed it and replied as pleasantly as she could. "Yes, thank you, Mrs. Tanner, I did know . . ." Not pleasant enough, for the start of an academic year. "But I have to admit," she said, rallying, "that I would never have thought of such a thing in the ordinary way. Hardly anyone in my classes has ever used a walking foot to quilt, so I've been trying to remember . . . They're quite expensive—forty or fifty pounds, I believe, so I know there was only one . . . I think it was the Burdena."

She had almost to sprint across to the grey, streamlined case to reach it before Lois could stake her claim. "If the rest of the class will excuse me, I'll just check this is the right one." Her hands beat those of Lois to the cover clips by the splittest of seconds, and now it was the eyes of Mrs. Tanner that glinted with annoyance.

"Ah, yes." Mrs. Franklin rummaged knowledgeably among the contents of a small, sleek, plastic box and, ignoring such lesser attachments as the binder, the buttonholer, the tucker, and the adjustable hemmer, swooped in triumph on the foot in question. "I was right: it was the Burdena."

"And it's the only walking foot they've got?"

Gladys tried not to feel affronted by Mrs. Tanner's tone. "As far as I can remember," she reiterated calmly, "yes. There's certainly very little call for a walking foot at school level. . . ." And then she couldn't help herself. "Besides, I imagine anybody doing the sort of work that would justify the cost is expected to have her own."

Lois ignored the echo of her own ironic inflections. "As you say, a walking foot doesn't come cheap. Unless anyone can be confident they're able to make proper use of one. Fifty pounds . . ."

Gladys allowed her eyebrows to arch in polite surprise.

"Surely, for an expert—the risk is minimal?" The pause was just long enough to make the point. Lois took it; and her cheeks grew pink before she decided it might be wiser to end the conversation with an attempt at a joke.

"I wonder what the tax man would say if I claimed it as an allowable expense before I *knew* I could use it! You know how it is when you're self-employed, Mrs. Franklin. All the grovelling and complicated explanations you have to keep making. So tiresome."

Gladys, accepting the plump woman's olive branch for the slender twig she knew it to be, was still obliged to acknowledge its truth. She nodded, but her smile was thin. She was wasting far too much time on Lois Tanner and her walking-foot nonsense, when she had a whole class waiting: a class entitled to her full attention and being, through no fault of her own, neglected. Now it was Gladys who flushed with embarrassment, but, before she could turn her attention to her other pupils, Lois spoke again.

"Then if it's all right with everybody, I'll be using the Burdena each week. Until I've got the hang of it." Like Mrs. Franklin, Lois knew the value of the significant pause; and, knowing it, only Gladys of all who now heard her could appreciate the difference between subtle emphasis and empty afterthought. Mrs. Tanner (Mrs. Franklin would bet herself a considerable sum) had no intention of buying her own walking foot while she could work on the Burdena once a week for no greater cost than the class fee, already paid.

"You see," said Lois, giving none of her audience the chance to respond to her assumption of privilege, "I've had the most marvellous idea for a design—*Starshimmer Moonscape*—which is simply crying out to be quilted in satin, and a walking foot is by far the best way to do it. It's a wall-hanging. Black and midnight blue for the sky, with appliqué sequins in silver, and diamanté specks, and wisps of sparking gauze for the stars, and the earth a huge, pale sapphire in the distance. Shades of pearl—cream and grey and ashes-of-roses—for the moon's surface, except the shadows of the craters, which I'll do in charcoal. A rainbow in the foreground, very faint, woven out of the earth-gleam reflected from the sun—borrowed light, you see, and the ghost of a rainbow, not the real thing but a barren echo of the world we know. . . ."

And her lyric flight was such that nobody had the nerve to dispute the claim of Lois Tanner to exclusive use of the Burdena and the attachment that would fit it, and no other, machine, week after week after week . . .

Until . . .

Deirdre Pollard had begun by making cushion covers, just to see if she could. With the minimum of assistance from Mrs. Franklin, she found that, for a beginner, she could; and very well indeed. She progressed swiftly from plain squares to squares with piped edges, and from tape ties to invisible zips. She learned how to stitch a neat French seam, and how to reverse it for upholstery purposes; she was initiated into the mysteries of cutting cloth on the bias; she mastered the art of self-covered buttons; she made pom-poms, wound tassels, and safety sewed great lengths of fringe without once tangling it in the feeder jaws of the machine.

Halfway through the year, she took Mrs. Franklin to one side. "This may sound daft, but . . . do you think I'm up to tackling a set of loose covers for my three-piece suite? It's why I came to classes in the first place," she explained as Gladys could only stare. "But—well . . ."

Mrs. Franklin came out of her trance. She smiled. "My dear Mrs. Pollard, you mustn't be so modest. I would have thought the answer was obvious! I was just wondering where we could find room in the town hall for one of your chairs, if you could spare it, once you'd finished the covers, for of course you must put your work on display with all the rest. I'm sure," she said as Deirdre looked pleased, "you'll do a splendid job. What material had you in mind? What sort of colour scheme?"

The conversation had thereafter become technical. Mrs. Franklin suggested that Mrs. Pollard should use a camera and her own judgement in combination with the colour wheel, a photocopied version of which she could let her have for a small sum. Any old sheets or similar large breadths of fabric could be used to make sample covers; she recommended the purchase of extra-long pins and strong tacking thread, both of which . . .

With one exception the rest of the class had followed Deirdre's upholstery endeavours with much interest. Alan Harvey (whose Boy Scout mentality of Making Do, coupled with his wife's insistence that he lose weight, had inspired him to try tailoring) declared that once he'd achieved the Norfolk jacket for which his soul craved, he would have a stab at a small marquee, or at the very least a bell-tent. As Alan, despite his best efforts, for all the patient guidance of Gladys Franklin, was still learning how to patch pockets, the marquee seemed a great way off; but the general laughter was kindly—with, again, one exception.

This exception was, of course, Lois Tanner. Lois took life seriously. She had not come to classes to have fun; she saw no point in struggling, week after week, with something you would never be any good at. And, in her heart, she envied Jean Harvey the husband who bicycled straight from his shift at the electrical works just to be with his wife, and who was happy to go supperless while she smocked tiny garments for their grandchildren, and gossiped with the many new friends she had made.

Husband! Lois had her suspicions: but she had no proof. Nicholas and Marianne. Her loving spouse, and her business partner. A change in alliance? A betrayal of trust? After so long, it was unthinkable. And yet . . .

One sultry afternoon Nicholas Tanner's once-trusting wife succumbed to a headache and went home early, leaving Marianne Gordon, divorcée, alone in their jointly owned shop. It was automatic for Lois to check the answering machine as soon as she entered the house, even if she sometimes felt disinclined to act until much later on what she heard . . . but what she heard this time did away with any inclination to leave things for later. It was little—but little enough: the tail end of a message which a subsequent, senseless message from the same person had not totally erased . . . and Lois recognised, only too well, the voice of the one who had left those messages, and guessed why she had done so.

She picked up the telephone and dialled. The receiver was picked up at the other end. Lois recognised, only too well, the voice of the one who answered.

"Stitcherie. Marianne speaking. How may I help you?"

"Marianne—Lois." The effort to sound normal almost choked her. "Are you . . . managing okay? I feel . . . so much better for the fresh air, I can come back in. If you want me." *Joke. With a choice of two who lived in the Tanner household and used the Tanner answering machine, it certainly wasn't Lois dear Marianne wanted.*

"This late in the day? Come off it. Of course I'm glad you aren't in bed with an ice pack on your head, but there's no need to push your luck. You shouldn't overdo things in such awful weather. I can manage fine on my own. . . ."

Curious that, in all the years she'd known her, Lois had never remarked the calculating note that sometimes entered Marianne's voice. As it did now.

"But, Lois, are you sure *you* can manage on your own? You said something about Nick working late, didn't you? Well, you oughtn't to be alone if you're planning to put your feet up. Suppose somebody comes to the door while you're trying to rest?" A pause. "I'd be happy to ring him for you."

I'm sure you would. "Goodness, there's no need to make such a fuss. I'm okay. I told you." *And I'm damned if I'm thanking you for the offer.* "In fact, I think I might be able to make my evening class after all—so don't worry. Even if I do start feeling ill again, I won't be on my own." *And neither will you. Or Nicholas. But not because he's working late. . . .*

Despite her aching heart and wounded pride, Lois felt a surge of pleasure for the way she had contrived to mislead Marianne with such minimal distortion of the truth. If her partners—either of them—were playing her false, she at least would scorn to tell a lie. Marianne might well have *inferred* something from what had been said . . . but could Lois be blamed for that? She had said only that she had *thought she might be able* to attend her evening class. . . .

But Lois Tanner did not attend her evening class—the first she had missed since the start of the academic year in October. For once, she had more important matters on her mind than the progress of *Starshimmer Moonscape*. There had, admittedly, been a brief hesitation as, crossing from one side of the St. Catherine's grounds to the other, she passed by the main buildings. She could see the lights of the crowded needlework room, could hear the voices of her fellow students drifting from the wide-open windows. Yet only the slightest stumble betrayed her doubts, and she was soon herself again, purposefully making her way along the public footpath past the new theatre towards the home of her faithless partner, confident that Nicholas and Marianne, whatever they might be doing, now or later, would not expect to have an unseen witness while they did it.

If, indeed, they did. Suspicion wasn't enough: she had to have proof. For all her boasted direct approach to life, she somehow baulked at trying to ambush the pair in flagrante. She was afraid of what she might do, of how she might react; and she despised herself for her weakness even as she reassured herself that it couldn't be a sign of weakness if she was prepared to spend all night at the bottom of Marianne's garden to find out what was really going on. She was being strong by insisting on fair play and the benefit of the doubt . . . and she wasn't afraid of being alone. After all, she might have to get used to it before long; it would be a test of her nerve for the trials that might lie ahead. And in such warm weather, she would come to little harm, sheltered by trees and shrubs, with a full moon to light her way, drowning out the stars . . .

"Starshimmer Moonscape." Gladys Franklin had wondered greatly when, after herself, Lois hadn't been the next to arrive at the needlework room, as she'd always been before. Lois never lost a chance of reinforcing her claim to the most modern machine in the room, and it wasn't like her to risk leaving her satin quilt uncompleted, so near the end of term and the week of the Allingham Exhibition. Her hanging, as she had frequently reminded everyone, would be a centrepiece for the class display. "She would have let us know, surely, if something had come up? I don't remember that she said last week she'd be away today. . . ."

"She didn't," said Deirdre Pollard, edging towards the Burdena with her arms full of heavy brocatelle fabric in a rich gold shade. "But as she's never this late normally—and with my loose covers so nearly finished—I'd love the chance to try her machine, just for a change."

"This machine," said Gladys with a hint of testiness, "is as much yours as it's Mrs. Tanner's, since it belongs to the school. Besides, Mrs. Tanner is lost past the plain quilting stage, from what I've seen. If you'd like to use it this evening, why don't you? Unless," she said with a mischievous glance round at the others, "anyone else would care to try before you start. Mr. Harvey? Your tweed, you know, might be far easier to feed through the Burdena. . . ."

The only person to laugh louder at Mrs. Franklin's little joke than Alan Harvey was Jean, long-suffering wife of the scoutmaster's bosom. On her husband's behalf, she ceded all rights in the Burdena to Mrs. Pollard, whose need—like her ability—was far greater than his.

"Wouldn't be hard," returned the jovial spouse, with a grin for his wife and a wink for Deirdre. "Carry on, Mrs. Pollard! We can't wait to see how it turns out."

And it turned out so well that, the following week, when Lois again showed no sign of coming to class, it was almost by instinct that Deirdre had settled herself and her yards of costly brocatelle in front of the Burdena. Nobody had disputed her right to use the machine. Mrs. Franklin, for once a more than late arrival, nodded amiably in Deirdre's direction, and was too busy with her apologies to say more. Everyone else was too busy with their particular projects to pay her any close attention. . . .

With the result that not a single member of the class noticed the ultimate—and furious—appearance of Lois Tanner until she had erupted into that tempestuous scene which, a week later, was to be of such interest to Trewley and Stone.

Eight

THE TEACHER MUST take full responsibility for her class, which responsibility had to include the behaviour of its various members while under her authority. . . .

Gladys Franklin dropped her gaze beneath the full force of the superintendent's bulldog glare. Sergeant Stone could have told her that Trewley intended his expression to radiate professional, but kindly, encouragement: she had never told *him* that it did not. She accepted that he did his best, but with features so darkly corrugated that station irreverents referred to him behind his back as the Plainclothes Prune, it must be an uphill task at the best of times. Which investigation of violent death seldom was . . .

Full responsibility for her class? But circumstances, Gladys reminded herself as she stared at the restless fingers on her lap, alter cases. This was a class of adults, not children. Even if—well, if some of them might have behaved like children; but, in a case of—she flinched—violent death . . .

"It was really very awkward, Superintendent," she said at last. "So embarrassing—and all my fault, I suppose you could say. In a way," she added as the bulldog rumbled his surprise. "Because if I hadn't spent so long fixing my car the previous week, maybe Mrs. Pollard wouldn't have . . . that is, two weeks running was perhaps a little . . ."

"Pushing my luck?" supplied Deirdre with a rueful grin as Gladys ran out of steam and Trewley, glancing about him, invited others to take up the tale. "Well, I suppose it was—but whoever would have thought the woman had such a temper on her? Nobody objects to a bit of plain speaking, but some people ought to think twice before saying what they think." She frowned. "Three times, even— and even then bite their tongues."

"This weather," said Alan Harvey peaceably, "we're all a bit twitchy—"

"That's what you call it? Biting my head off and making a regular exhibition of herself and being so—so scathing about my work? *Twitchy?*" Mrs. Pollard let out an exasperated snort. At another time she might have hurled the how-like-a-man observation at him as well. "The understatement of the year, that is. Lois Tanner is—I mean, was . . ."

"Hot," supplied Scoutmaster Harvey, doing his good deed for the day as Deirdre turned white with the shock of sudden recollection. "Mrs. Tanner was understandably hot and bothered and tired from hurrying to get here on time, and being pretty sure she'd be late anyway, and . . ."

"And," went on his wife as he paused for breath, "from finding when she got here that indoors was almost as hot as she was, with one of the fans not working, and the place cluttered all over with stepladders while the janitor tried to fix it—"

"Only one ladder," her husband corrected her gently. "It was just unlucky that . . ."

There was another pause. Trewley broke it. "Unlucky? Black cats and pinch-of-salt stuff, you mean?" Trewley, son of Allshire, had an ambivalent attitude towards superstition. "Harbingers of doom type of thing? Or a bit more down-to-earth, like this janitor dropped a spanner on the poor woman's head?"

As everyone shuffled silently over who should answer him, he chuckled. "I've often thought there must be the start of it. Some bloke walks under a ladder, bloke up it with a paint-pot sneezes: bingo! Much safer to walk round the thing next time. That what happened last week?"

"The caretaker," he was informed after a few moments by a crisp-voiced Avis Thoday, "gives the impression of being a very competent young man: hardly the type to allow things to fall from a ladder on which he was working. And, if indeed he had, and had anyone been injured, I would have expected, as headmistress of the school, to be informed of the fact." Her gaze flicked keenly from Gladys Franklin to Kathleen Shorey, and back. "Since no such incident was in fact reported, one must assume—"

"Your assumption," broke in Gladys, "is correct." This cool commandeering by the still-new head of Mrs. Franklin's small authority had stiffened the spine of the needlecraft teacher. "The only . . . incident to occur at my class last week was that poor Mrs. Pollard was subjected to what can only be described as a—a torrent of abuse from Mrs. Tanner, who then turned her attentions to me when I observed that I could see no reason why, since she had arrived so late, she should not use another machine just this once." Her chin rose, and she met Trewley's interested regard with a look of bravado. "I pointed out that many people actually *prefer* to quilt without using any foot at all—as I myself do—and that it is a most useful technique to acquire."

She turned pink as one or two of those who had witnessed the response of Lois to this well-meant suggestion suppressed their amusement. "How was I to know," she demanded, "that Mrs. Tanner had already tried at home, and was quite unable to master the basic control skills? If she had only explained at the start that her insistence on using the Burdena every week was because . . . But there was no need for her to be so—so extremely rude," she concluded, blushing more than ever. "Plain speech is one thing, but . . ."

Trewley observed numerous nodding heads and sympathetic looks among the needlecraft students. It was clear that, though shocked by what had happened, few people had much kind feeling to spare for the late Lois Tanner; he wondered whether they'd had all that much before. Was Stone's theory that the woman might have tried touting for custom among her fellow pupils so very credible? The more he found out about the unlamented Lois, the less likely it seemed.

"Troublesome things, sewing machines," he remarked as he rose to his feet. "Oh, I've heard my wife once or twice, when she hasn't known I'm there: a surprising turn of phrase she's got, for a respectable married woman. Setting sleeves and fitting zips and getting hems straight—a difficult business, right enough. And with anything too fancy— and in hot weather like we've had this past month . . . Well, folk are bound to say a bit more than they really mean, from time to time. I've no doubt," Trewley added, with a kindly grin for Gladys and a nod for the pale Mrs. Pollard, "you both gave her as good as you got, and I'd quite understand if you said you did—and I'd be a bit surprised," he said as they opened their mouths to protest, "if you tried telling me you didn't. It's only human nature to stand up for yourself—and she can't have minded that much, can she? Seeing as she came back to class again this week, I mean. Just as if nothing had happened." The bulldog suddenly lowered his head to direct a piercing gaze upon every member of the class in turn.

"Only then it did," he added, following what had seemed like the longest pause in history. "Happen." Another lengthy pause. Even Avis Thoday held her breath. "Which is why, now you've all started remembering so nicely, I'm leaving you to some of my officers who'll listen to what you remember and take it down for me to read back at the station. You'll be wanting to get off home as soon as you can: a cup of tea, a bit of peace and quiet on your own territory, and perfectly understandable, in the circumstances." He rumbled with what was meant to be kindly laughter. "As for me and the sergeant here . . . could be we'll be seeing some of you later. But for now, if you'll excuse us . . ."

And, with a nod for PC Benson to alert the rest of the team to proceed in routine fashion, Superintendent Trewley and his sidekick made their exit from the room.

THE THIRD UNANSWERED ring confirmed their suspicions that nobody was at home. While Trewley remained, just in case, on the doorstep, Stone slipped around the side of the house to check the garden for a deckchair-drowsing Nicholas Tanner: but she was back in a few moments, shaking her head.

"We could try—" began Trewley, but was interrupted.

"While the cat's away," came a sardonic voice from the other side of the fence, "the rat's at play." A tall, more than slim, faded russet blonde with blank eyes and a sour expression had evidently been a silent witness of events for some minutes past.

"You won't find him here," she went on before Trewley could speak, "not if it's Nick you want—and dear Lois is at her evening class. Which explains why Nick isn't home, either." Her lips twisted derisively. "Not at home *here*, I mean, though I imagine very much at home where he *is*, thank you." She shook the pale tawny locks away from her face and swayed a little as she leaned towards the detectives as they made their way down the path. "You wonder how he finds the energy in this weather—but rats are hardy creatures, I'm told. Look at the ones who have developed an immunity to poison." Something like a snigger escaped her before she went on. "If Lois wants him out of her hair, she'll have to do rather better than arsenic in the soup."

She winked grotesquely as she raised a hand—glittering with bracelets about the wrist, with rings on all four scarlet-tipped fingers—across her mouth. "Goodness, I suppose I shouldn't really be talking like this to you, should I?" She didn't even try to sound perturbed. "Don't tell me," she begged, mock-horrified. "They've found Nick and

Marianne bludgeoned to death in the master bedroom, and you want to arrest dear Lois for taking the law into her own hands!" Solemnly she shook her head. "You'll have to try someone else, you know. I may not like the woman—I can't think of anyone who does—but I won't"—she put her hand on her heart—"say a word against anyone who rids the world of a cheating husband. Whether she did it herself or paid a hit man, they only got what was coming to them, in my opinion. And high time they got it, too!"

Trewley and Stone were in reflective mood as at last they contrived to escape their loquacious new acquaintance. They had politely declined to enlarge on their wish to speak with Nicholas Tanner; they had announced that if the house of Marianne Gordon was indeed the address where he was most likely to be found, then to the house of Marianne Gordon they would go. No; while they appreciated the offer, they would prefer not to wait next door until either Mr. or—the merest hesitation—Mrs. Tanner returned. In fact, they had better be on their way at once. . . .

"Gin," said Trewley as the car rumbled along through the deepening dusk. "At a guess. Seeing we never really got near enough to smell her breath, I mean."

Stone wrinkled her nose reminiscently. "You could be right, sir. She must have been knocking back some kind of booze. Nobody in full possession of her senses gardens, or whatever she thought she was doing, dripping with that much jewellery, whether it was top-notch Bond Street or costume. I didn't spot a glass, though, did you?"

The superintendent grunted. The sergeant fell silent. The car continued on its way, Stone changing from sidelights to dipped as the trees lining the roads along which they passed arched ever higher into a gracefully darkening sky.

Even veiled in deepening twilight, the house of Marianne Carmel Gordon, business partner to Lois Tanner and rumoured mistress to Nicholas of that ilk, was surprisingly close in age, style and appearance to that which Trewley and Stone had just left. "What d'you bet," muttered Stone as the pair made their way up the path, "he's hoping to trade in his wife for a younger model?" She coughed. "Was, I mean. But you know how some men are, sir. The mid-life urge to rejuvenate. If Mrs. Gordon has black hair, too, and is a bit on the plump side . . ."

Trewley pressed his thumb on the doorbell. "Sergeant, you've got an altogether jaundiced view of the opposite sex. Can't think why. I'd've said young What's-His-Name was as reliable as they make 'em, yet here you are, shattering my illusions—"

Then he shut up as the patter of light, swift footsteps grew loud around the side of the house. They were echoed, he was intrigued to note, by a heavier, more wary tread that came to a halt—he would guess—just out of sight, the treader standing invisible guard as the owner of the less heavy feet appeared in view.

Stone caught her breath in a gasp of irritated satisfaction as the newcomer proved, indeed, to bear a more than distant similarity to the late Lois Tanner. She was too professional, however, to voice her satisfaction aloud as her superior greeted the black-haired beauty in the manner decreed by law.

Marianne inspected the warrant cards closely, taking them closer to the road—and, the detectives noted, farther from the still-unseen guard—and to the streetlight on the pavement outside her front garden. "Very well," she said, sounding puzzled. "Superintendent Trewley, Sergeant Stone—what can you possibly want with me?"

Trewley cleared his throat, glanced pointedly over his shoulder at neighbouring houses, and observed that it was rather a private matter. If they might speak to Mrs. Gordon indoors, it would make things easier, he thought.

"Oh." Mrs. Gordon frowned. Trewley waited. Marianne, with a sigh, glanced at what she could see of his face by the street lamp's glow, and gave in. "Oh, very well." She sighed again as she led the way back up the path, raising her voice as she added: "I hope this won't take too long. I'm rather busy just now. Still, as a law-abiding citizen, I know it's my duty to help the police, so . . ."

She had done her best to warn her invisible guardian, but couldn't completely mask the scuffle of presumably retreating feet as whoever it was did a swift vanishing act into the gloom. The little party made its way around the side of the house—Marianne hesitated carefully beside the front door before remarking with a laugh that of course it was locked from the inside—and stepped into the soft golden glow of dimmed lights falling through open French windows upon a flagstone patio, set with comfortable garden furniture including long, plump-cushioned loungers close together, with a table of drinks between them.

"We'll go into the sitting room," said Marianne quickly as her visitors seemed inclined to linger in the open air. "Since you say it's so important and official, perhaps . . ."

A bulldog, once its mind is made up, can be impossible to shift from its chosen stance. Trewley's ears had heard the sound of those invisible feet; his eyes had seen the evidence of the invisible one's intimacy with his hostess. If he wanted to linger, then linger he would. He stopped dead in his tracks and peered into the garden shadows.

"Of course, if Mr. Tanner would care to join us now, it'd save time having to find him later." He ignored the little cry from the woman silhouetted in the doorway, the sudden indignant babblings of denial. He turned to glower in the general direction of the startled vegetable rustle that his words seemed to have provoked. "If you'd be so kind, Mr. Tanner."

It was not an invitation.

Nine

NICHOLAS TANNER, ONCE he emerged into the light, proved to be a good-looking, rather rakish character in his middle forties. He had an easy manner and a ready smile. He would, Stone decided, make the perfect confidence trickster, the type to fancy himself a ladies' man: the type to charm the older ones, and succeed with the younger ones. If they didn't keep their wits about them.

"Since you insist, Superintendent." Wisely Nicholas made no pretense that he hadn't listened with interest to everything that had already passed. Carefully, before entering the house, he wiped free of imaginary dew the shoes in which he had crossed the heat-dried lawn from the shrubbery. "I do trust this . . . official visit is not in the nature of a raid?"

"No, sir." There was no echoing smile in Trewley's tone as he replied. Nicholas, looking faintly puzzled, smiled again in a man-of-the-world way. "Come now, Superintendent, the moral majority is all very well—but what happens in the privacy of someone's home can hardly be anything to do with the police. This is a democracy, for goodness' sake. A free society. Mrs. Gordon and I have committed no crime. We're both consenting adults—and nobody could exactly accuse us of frightening the horses."

"No, sir," said Trewley again. Nicholas couldn't tell whether he had missed the Mrs. Patrick Campbell quotation altogether, or whether he had chosen to ignore it. "It's rather more serious than . . . a spot of rustling." Trewley glanced from Nicholas to Marianne. "I think it would be better if we all sat down."

Something about the way he said this made Marianne obey without demur. As she sank into a chair, she looked only once at Nicholas, then kept her eyes fastened on Trewley's face; Nicholas, confused, found himself watching Stone as she selected an upright chair with padded arms, and quietly took a notepad from her pocket.

"We've bad news for you, I'm afraid," Trewley said. He always hated this part. As far as he was concerned, there was only one way to break bad news, and that was quickly. It wasn't kind to wrap it up; it just prolonged the agony. After one sympathetic look, he stared resolutely between the two faces facing him at the ornate fabric folderol on the wall. Something from Stitcherie, he shouldn't wonder.

"Bad news for both of you, in fact. Your wife, Mr. Tanner—your partner, Mrs. Gordon—I'm sorry to say that something has happened to her." It was only a slight distortion of the facts. "Something . . . serious." If he hadn't had it before, now he had their full attention. "And—she's dead." Plain facts: no distortion this time.

Marianne's black hair framed a face all at once as stark white as the lace that decorated the hanging on the wall behind her. Deep furrows hollowed her cheeks as the skin stretched suddenly tight over her bones: every muscle in her body had contracted in shock. On her knees, her hands were curled into tortured balls. Stone hoped that her nails were not too long; she shuddered to think of the likely damage to the older woman's palms.

"Something's happened to Lois? An accident?" Nicholas shook his head. "There must be some mistake. She's the most careful driver in the world. . . ." He saw that Trewley, with no spirit of mockery, was likewise shaking his head. He hesitated. "But I suppose if some drunk . . ." His eyes, darting from side to side of the room, came to focus on the sideboard clock. "No, it's barely chucking-out time. It wouldn't have happened before—and how could you have been here so soon?" He sat up straight; his shoulders relaxed. "No, it can't be Lois. I won't believe it!"

Trewley said: "I'm sorry, sir, you must. Your wife Lois is dead. And I'm sorry, again, if I've given you the wrong impression, but it wasn't a road accident. It happened up at the school."

"The school?" Nicholas frowned. "She was at her class this evening, that's true. . . ."

Even at such a moment he couldn't help the way his eyes flicked sideways to where Marianne sat, the colour slowly returning to her cheeks as she began to revive. Her breath, which had been ragged and uneven, was calmer, and the white-knuckled fists she had made of her hands had unclenched.

She felt his glance on her, and the colour in her cheeks deepened to a blush. She dropped her gaze, then raised her head in quiet defiance and spoke.

"Poor Nick." Her voice quivered. "And poor, poor Lois. What dreadful news . . . but how on earth did it happen? A—a fatal accident at a needlework class? It doesn't make sense." She took care not to catch Nicholas's eye. "Unless somebody stabbed her with a pair of shears, I mean, or hit her over the head with a bolt of cloth—but then it would hardly be an accident, would it?"

Trewley did not wish to correct the mistake just yet. If it was indeed a genuine mistake, and not merely somebody trying to be too clever. He hadn't missed the way she'd not liked to look in the husband's direction when she'd decided to push the anyone-might-have-wanted-to-kill-the-wife idea. Did she suspect that Nicholas knew more about it than he was letting on? Or were they in it together?

"You don't sound too surprised at the idea that someone might have wanted to harm Mrs. Tanner," he observed. "The type of person to drive folk to violence, was she? Passions running high among the crochet hooks and samplers?"

Marianne achieved an anxious little gasp. "Oh, Superintendent, you surely can't suspect *me* of wishing Lois any harm!" Now she contrived a pretty smile. "Honestly, you don't work in close partnership with someone for more than eight years unless you both agree about—well, the fundamentals. I can't say we're—that we *were*," she amended with a sigh, "the best of bosom friends, because that wouldn't be true." Once more she avoided giving any indication that Lois's husband was sitting close to her. "But we never had any *serious* disagreements—and," she said with another pretty smile and a gentle laugh, "all this is academic, isn't it? Accidents will happen, and of course I'm sorry—but I still don't quite see *how*. She was sewing, not doing gym. Did she slip, or trip on a sewing machine cable, and fall?"

"Lois," said Nicholas, before Trewley could reply, "is—*was*—hardly the type to go tripping over cables and—and bumping her head, or whatever she did. You know what she was like, she never missed a thing. If somebody left a wire lying around where it shouldn't have been, she'd have gone after them with all guns blazing until they coiled it safely out of the way before anyone less . . . less *noticing* could trip over it." There was a curious mixture of the pejorative and the scornful in his tone as he remarked on Lois's powers of observation. Whatever else his wife might have noticed, it seemed her husband had successfully fooled her about his extramarital concerns. . . .

Or, wondered Trewley . . . had he?

"Whatever it was," concluded Nicholas, for the first time allowing a hint of uncertainty to enter his voice, "I'm sure it was nothing like that. . . ." He licked his lips and favoured Trewley with a questioning look. "What . . . what *did* happen to Lois, Superintendent?"

Marianne expressed the same sentiment, but quietly and with more grace than her presumed lover. Either she was acting, or she did feel some genuine emotion at the death of her business partner and former friend: but the emotion (whatever it might be) was—in the same way as that eventually shown by Nicholas—not deep. Trewley supposed the pair had accepted that he, like the rest of Allingham, must know pretty much all there was to know, or to guess, about their relationship. Top marks for lack of hypocrisy: score low for tact—and perhaps, depending on what might happen later, for common sense, as well.

"It seems," he said slowly, "there was a fault with the . . . with the sewing machine your wife always used."

"The Burdena?" It was Marianne who spoke. "A fault? But it was the latest model! That's why she insisted on using it, because of the quilting foot. I could understand if it had been one of the older machines, but—"

"But it was the Burdena," said Trewley, grateful to her for having reminded him. "And she was"—he tried not to wince—"electrocuted. It would have been very quick," he added as both Nicholas and Marianne uttered startled exclamations, "so the medical people say." Not that he planned to go into details. "Instantaneous. Believe me, she would never have known anything about it."

Only now, with the eyes of the two detectives upon him, did Nicholas gear himself up for the big scene he must suddenly have grasped that he should have enacted the instant the news had been broken. . . .

Marianne, suspected Stone (who always tried to give her fellow females the benefit of the doubt, hard though this sometimes was) would have made a better job of it.

"Electrocuted? Lois? How . . . how horrible!" His eyes widened, his face quivered, his voice shook. "That damned foot! If only she'd learned how to do without it—but she tried, she couldn't, she wouldn't accept second best—that was Lois, a perfectionist—conscientious to a fault—never anything half-hearted about her . . . whatever she did, she did! How can you sit there and say she wouldn't have known a thing about it? What difference does that make to the—the awful, senseless waste of it all? Lois! I think I'm going mad!"

He buried his head in his hands and sobbed aloud.

• • •

"So HOW DID you like the performance, sir?" enquired Stone as they finally drove away from Marianne's house, leaving Nicholas (whose tearful face it had been the sergeant's great pleasure to slap) under sedation prescribed by the emergency doctor summoned by an equally tearful—were those tears any more genuine?—Marianne.

Trewley, mopping his brow, snorted. "Took him a while to get going, but he didn't do such a bad job, in the end."

"With a little help from his friends," muttered Stone.

Trewley snorted again. "Yes, well, I don't reckon either of 'em really cared tuppence for the poor woman." He rubbed his chin, frowning. "Mind you, from what we've heard so far, I'm not sure I'd have been that keen on her myself." He brooded on his wife, his three daughters, and the energetic sergeant at his side. "Can't abide these bossy women who always know best—but it doesn't make them murderers, Stone," he concluded as she audibly ground her teeth. "The husband and the girlfriend, I mean. No matter how much she might have annoyed them."

"No matter how much one or other or both of them might have wanted her out of the way, sir," prompted Stone. "I take it we'll be looking into the business arrangements at Stitcherie tomorrow?"

His burgeoning yawn turned into a groan, and he began to sputter. Stone slowed the car. "Another midge? I'll wind the windows up—"

"No!" He choked himself into clarity. "No, thanks, we need all the fresh air we can get." Once more he mopped his brow. "If only it would rain . . ."

"Gosh, yes. I wouldn't even mind a thunderstorm, after this long. . . . But," she said smartly, "there must be *somebody* around who can explain the financial side of things without giving us both a headache, sir. Accountants—auditors—anyone who does it for a job shouldn't find the heat a particular problem, should they? Not like us."

Trewley was mopping his forehead again as the car

slowed for the turn into the police station. "You don't know how much I hope there is. I wouldn't want to sit down with columns of figures and a pocket calculator at the best of times, let alone in weather like this. Everyone stick to their own job, that's what I say. And ours," he said as the car came to a halt, and Stone prepared to reverse it into the parking space, "is catching whoever fixed that blasted sewing machine. If Benson and the rest have kept their wits about them, we ought to have a nice long list of names and addresses to work on. . . ."

"Tomorrow?" ventured Stone as he yawned again.

"Tomorrow," he agreed. "My brain's going to turn into mush if I don't get a few hours' sleep. . . ."

"IF YOU DON'T shut up and go to sleep this minute, I swear I'll murder you!"

It was midnight, and Julie Garner's throat was almost raw from screaming. The kids had done nothing all day but moan about how hot they were, how they were bored and uncomfortable, and it wasn't fair they couldn't go for a swim in the pool the way the girls did, when they'd all gone home and nobody would see, and Dad could take them, couldn't he, if Mum was mean enough to keep saying no . . .

"No," Craig had said when he'd popped in for a cup of tea, and the three of them started on at him before he'd had time to sit down. He spoke as if, for once, there was no room for argument. For once he'd backed Julie up, not sided with the kids like he usually did, causing her more trouble than she'd had in the first place. "You brats trying to bring me grief in my new job? We don't want to go upsetting that posh lot from school. Your mum's right, you can't have a swim—but," he said as they began to whine, "there ain't nothing to stop you paddling in the spinney pond, if you like. Nice cool mud between your toes, catch a few tiddlers—"

"Craig!" Julie's yell had effectively silenced the now

enthusiastic squeals of her offspring. "Don't you dare go putting such daft ideas in their heads! You trying to get them drowned? Poisoned from goodness-knows-what as lives in that filthy smelly water?" She gulped. She wished she hadn't thought of that. "You lot go anywhere near the pond and you'll feel the back of my hand." She swallowed. "Or worse—and don't say you weren't warned." She gasped. "And if you egg 'em on, Craig Garner—so help me— I'll . . ."

But she had been unable to continue. Clapping a hand to her mouth, she turned and bolted from the kitchen. Her husband and children heard the stumbling rush of her footsteps on the stairs, and tried not to listen to her tormented spasms as she was, for the umpteenth time that long, hot, weary day, sick into the bowl of the toilet.

In the kitchen Craig shuddered. His handsome face twisted with revulsion as he pushed his half-empty mug away. How could he be expected to drink his tea in peace with all this going on? What he wanted was out of this dump, away from his sickly, nagging cow of a wife—and there was the perfect excuse (as if anyone could blame him) sitting right in front of him, looking downright bloody miserable, poor little beggars, after a whole day stuck with her. . . .

"You're right, it's hot," he told the three youngsters. "Like I said, no swimming, but—anyone want to go for a walk before supper? A spot of fresh air'll do us all good, and we won't wait for mum." Anything to get clear before she pulled the chain and came down to join them. "She don't feel so good. She'll be glad of a bit o' peace and quiet with looking after you lot all day. . . ."

And when Julie had recovered herself enough to grope her way down the stairs, she found that she had been left quite alone in the cottage. This did not put her in a good mood. It wasn't enough for Craig, the bastard, not to care whether she happened to feel ill with his fourth bloody brat or not, but now he was teaching the other brats not to care, either. Dragging them off with him goodness-knew-where making them late for supper, bringing them home worn out with walking and playing daft games, she wouldn't wonder, overexcited and hungry and hot—and him, she'd bet a million, handing 'em over like Lord Muck to the scullery maid for her to look after while he swanned off to the pub, or wherever it was he went most nights to meet his awful friends, and her having to feed and wash and deal with the little bleeders by herself, him being the last person to offer to help her. . . .

"So never mind swans," said Julie to the empty kitchen. "What's sauce for the bleeding goose is sauce for the bleeding gander! If Master Craig thinks I'm going to hang around here all night waiting for him to come home, he can think again. No law says I can't go for a walk, too, is there?"

She had gone.

She had vanished. The grounds of St. Catherine's school were spacious and well landscaped, with clumps of trees and knots of shrubbery as well as beds of flowers, and even a vegetable patch and a fruit garden, high-walled in mellow brick which soaked up the sun all year round.

It was to these gardens first that Julie made her angry way, for they were nothing to do with Craig. They were, under the auspices of the biology mistress, the responsibility of Katies of the middle rank. Younger girls were deemed too small to dig; older girls were far too busy with exams. By the time each pupil left school at eighteen, she would, in theory, be able to run a smallholding single-handed, as well as a fair-sized house. The education offered by seven years at St. Catherine's was nothing if not all-round. . . .

And didn't it just *cost?* No expense spared for those bitches; nothing but the best for the pampered Daddy's Girls. A brand new theatre for their stupid school plays, a gym, a swimming pool—heated, as if anyone needed it warm in weather like this . . .

Julie's solitary, brooding walk did nothing to improve her temper. Nor did it help that, when she finally decided to go

home, it was to find Craig had come back, dumped the
kids—without feeding them, of course—and gone again.
They were, as she'd feared, worn out and hungry and hot,
and she'd been able to do nothing with them all evening.
She'd suffered for what seemed like hours . . .

And nobody in the little cottage managed a wink of sleep
all night.

——————— Ten ———————

TREWLEY'S LUCK WAS only a little better. His house stood halfway up a hill, its windows hopefully wide and welcoming to the relentlessly calm night air. The crime prevention officer in him had agonised long over the risks of illicit intrusion; the suffering human being couldn't find the energy to care. With his youngest daughter and her two best friends camped in a tent in the back garden, and a tangle of roses scaling a trellis up the front wall, he felt he might rest more or less easy in his bed—as he did, for a few, fitful hours.

They should have been more.

"You don't look too chirpy this morning, sir." Stone was already at her desk, poring over a pile of preliminary statements and sipping tea from a generous mug, when her superior lumbered in. Never at the best of times a snappy dresser, he now seemed positively unkempt in his tieless, open-necked state, the wrinkled shirt a cruel mockery of the grey, corrugated countenance. "Didn't you sleep well?"

"Did anyone in this benighted country? Believe me, if—Hey!" The bloodhound scowled and sniffed the air. "So that's what . . ." He turned to scowl in the direction of the filing cabinet, on the top of which stood a reproachful, fan-shaped lacuna. "Hell's bloody bells!"

"Er—yes, sir. I'm sorry. I did my best, but—"

The superintendent offered an opinion of Desk Sergeant Pleate which made Stone hide a smile, then collapsed on his chair, leaned his head back against the wall, and emitted a gusty sigh. "I suppose I can't touch *him*, but I could certainly murder a cup of tea."

Stone spoke with erudition of heat exhaustion, nocturnal restlessness, and the need for fluid replenishment. She did not offer to pop along to the canteen. The superintendent, whose normal approach to her liberated principles was one of teasing acceptance, sighed again.

"It was the drive here that finished me. Thought I'd beat the rush hour before it got too hot, but everyone else had the same blasted idea, of course. Then Pleate grabbed me about his damned Lost Property and—and *raids*, if you please, on that perishing cupboard, and—"

Stone made up her mind. "You read these," she said, handing him the statements she'd finished checking and the detailed notes she'd made. "I'll be back as soon as I can. I've, um, had the Official Talking-To already, sir, so even if he is in the canteen, I doubt if he'll pick on me twice in one morning, especially when he knows how busy we are."

He didn't. She returned safely less than five minutes later, bearing two large mugs on a tray. These she placed on Trewley's blotter, with the stern injunction that he must finish both of them if he didn't want to suffer dehydration, prostration, hypotension, and similar horrors. Obediently the superintendent raised a mug with one hand as he waved Stone's notebook in the other.

"Too many of the blighters," he said, and drank.

This cryptic observation was, of course, no particular mystery to Detective Sergeant Stone. "Far too many," she agreed, setting herself lightly on his visitors' chair and preparing to theorise. "Benson and the others have certainly been busy."

"Umph." Trewley addressed himself once more to his mug, motioning her to continue. She reached across the desk for her notebook, and leafed quickly through it.

"Mr. and Mrs. Harvey. Alan Harvey's an electrician, which for our purposes is quite bad enough without being a

Scoutmaster, too. Look how Boy Scouts are trained from birth to turn three bits of wood, an old tin can, and six inches of string into a bedside lamp in full working order. A man like that could switch a couple of wires with malice aforethought almost in his sleep."

Trewley winced, and stifled a yawn. "And Mrs.?"

"First-aid training does imply a practical turn of mind, and they've been married a long time. Jean Harvey could easily have picked up more than enough knowledge to make the switch by . . . well, a sort of marital osmosis, sir."

"I suppose when you give up the CID you'll try for a job in Traffic, then," said Trewley, while acknowledging that she had a point.

"The way you say I drive?" Stone raised her eyebrows, then directed her gaze sternly to the second mug of tea until, with a wry shrug, the superintendent picked it up. The sergeant returned to her notes. "Gladys Franklin. Teacher. Another practical mind: when her car threw a tantrum last week, she was able to fix it herself instead of having to call out the repair man."

Trewley thumped his empty mug on the desk. "Tantrums all over the show last week, weren't there? Her car doesn't start, teacher arrives late in a bit of a mood, and deceased arrives even later, to go hammer and tongs full blast at one of teacher's pet pupils . . ."

"Deirdre Pollard," supplied Stone with a shake of the head. "I suppose we should take it for granted she's practical-minded, too: anyone who can even contemplate making a set of fitted covers for a three-piece suite is hardly what I'd call a bumbler."

"Same here. And?"

"The two Lewises. Mother, Christine, is a housewife and proud of it—incidentally, she's a Katie. She'd know her way around the premises: where the spare keys are kept, and so on. That is, if we assume the needlework room was locked, as we're told it's always meant to be."

"Ascertain," said Trewley, "don't assume. That's one of the golden rules of detection, Stone."

"Yes, sir. It'll be checked today." She coughed gently. "The Lewis daughter, Sharon, is also a Katie, so the same applies to her. Some sort of computer programmer, living at home before she gets married." She wrinkled her nose at this quaint concept. "The classes are to make her wedding dress, sir. White lace, the full works, according to Benson—I never realised he knew so much about sewing."

"He's got four older sisters," said Trewley. "And his mother's a widow. Not much money. Your . . . family osmosis can work both ways, remember."

"Er—yes, sir. About Sharon: computers are certainly scientific, but I don't know how bright you have to be to program them. I believe some people just sit punching in numbers all day without needing to use their brains at all."

"No comment. And what does the father do?"

"A plumber." Again she shook her head. "I don't know how much of the osmosis thing would apply here. When we had the central heating replaced, I think our chap brought someone else in to wire the thermostat, but—"

"An old-fashioned setup. Not you and young What's-His-Name—but here's this girl, home saving for her bottom drawer, father out to work while mother does nothing but keep house—not, mind you, that that's not a hard day's work, if it's properly done. But it somehow isn't my idea of the modern woman." A chuckle rumbled deep in the bloodhound's throat, and his mighty jowls quivered. "Maybe I've been brainwashed by knowing too many modern women."

Stone chose to ignore him. "Another widow: Mrs. Clark. Making a crazy quilt, piecing it by machine in class to decorate by hand at home. She only comes for the company, she says. Benson seemed pretty impressed by the work she, um, apparently insisted on showing him, sir. The clear inference is that she's someone else who has nimble fingers and a practical mind."

"And a bossy streak in her, if she can bulldoze young

Benson—though that headmistress had him jumping, by all accounts, so maybe he's not as tough as I thought."

"I haven't even started on the school staff yet, sir." Stone indicated the reports still unread on her desk, then tapped her notebook with a pencil she had absently removed from the old marmalade jar in which her superior kept ballpoint pens, felt tips, and other writing implements together with a wicked paper knife he swore had been used to stab his predecessor-but-two. "I hadn't reached the last of the sewing class when you arrived. There must be a good half dozen after . . ." Once more she consulted her notebook. "Miss Winifred Ashley. Retired civil servant."

"Umph," observed Trewley as Stone paused significantly. "Yes, well, we've all done that on the odd occasion. I prefer 'government official,' myself—but she isn't one of us, Stone. Not unless she's retired here from somebody else's manor."

"A tax inspector, then," deduced Stone: to which deduction Trewley nodded in a sympathetic silence. "It's about the best conversation-stopper there is. 'Do tell me what,'" she began in the accents of a society matron, "'you do for a living.'" She adopted a funereal, guilt-laden tone. "'I'm afraid I work for the Inland Revenue.'" She flung up her hands in horror. "'Unclean, unclean! Never darken my doors again! Away with you to the bottomless pit!'"

Trewley gazed at her with some curiosity. "Interesting parties you must go to. Nothing of that sort's ever happened to me—but then, pretty well everyone knows me around here." He rolled lugubrious eyes to the ceiling. "Hardly a surprise, I suppose . . ."

Indeed it was not. There could be few faces in Allingham more memorable. Corrugated like a year's supply of cardboard boxes, resembling a much-crumpled, large-scale Ordnance Survey map dropped in a puddle and dried under a mattress, the unique features of Detective Superintendent Trewley had a weatherbeaten, lived-in look for which Central Casting must have scoured the country in vain for a second Policeman, long service, wide experience, tenacious, successful, and world-weary.

"Miss Ashley," he was informed, "is making a layette for her sister's latest granddaughter. Her pension doesn't run to buying things any more, and she's into self-sufficiency in a big way. She apparently thought it would be fun"—Stone's manner suggested that she did not share this opinion—"to sew the whole thing on the treadle machine, because it's almost exactly the same as the one her grandmother used to have, though she appreciates that this is a little sentimental of her." She sighed. "Of course, self-sufficiency *might* just mean growing her own vegetables or keeping chickens or bees, but . . ."

Trewley rolled his eyes again, this time turning the look of accusing despair directly upon his sergeant. "Didn't I tell you so? There's too many of the blighters—far too many. And it'll take Lord knows how many man-hours and more to check every single one of them. . . ."

It was not an observation calculated to inspire.

THROUGHOUT THE WHOLE of that day, the routine of police investigation was pursued with dogged determination. Witnesses were interviewed, notes were taken, reports were compiled and delivered to Trewley's office, where he and Stone caught up with them after their return from a more detailed talk, in the presence of his solicitor, with Nicholas Tanner.

Nicholas had been happy to remain in a state of sedated shock, safe from the risks of interrogation, until he found out that the police had returned to talk not to him, but to Marianne. It was, of course, her house: it was the logical place for them to pursue their enquiries with Mrs. Gordon, business partner of the murdered woman. But Nicholas chose to assume an attitude of extreme chivalry which might better have been adopted, on her behalf, during Lois Tanner's lifetime. He leaped from his sickbed, erupted into the sitting room, and insisted that neither Marianne nor he would answer a single question without first having obtained the benefit of legal advice.

"He's a downy one," grumbled Trewley as he sat with Stone in their office, drinking tea and fanning themselves with the typewritten pages of numerous reports. "Knows his way around, does Master Nicholas. The question is, was he keeping quiet on his own account, or was he boxing clever to stop her saying anything she shouldn't?"

"Neither of them said anything much at all," Stone said regretfully. "Of course, they had plenty of time beforehand to work out their alibis. If they needed them," she added, conscientious as Lois Tanner herself would, according to report, have been. "The field's still wide open—though it isn't quite as wide as it was this morning, if we believe the Lewis pair when they say they left home and travelled to St. Catherine's together. Whoever hocussed that machine did it after the last, um, official class of the school day: the girl who used it then didn't come to any harm, did she?"

"Windows of opportunity," grumbled Trewley. "Timetables—you don't know how I hate 'em." Stone was wise enough not to remind him that she in fact did, having heard him on the subject more than several times before. "Process of elimination be damned! Give me good honest policing any day. Something I can get my teeth into without all this infernal paper-pushing nonsense . . ."

"We'll just have to talk to everyone again tomorrow," said Stone, taking the knife out of her pocket to sharpen her pencil in readiness. "In person, I mean, not just reading the reports. You know as well as I do, sir, that sooner or later somebody's bound to give something away. Sooner or later, something will happen. . . ."

And then she jumped, and dropped the open knife, as something did.

On Trewley's paper-piled desk, the telephone rang. . . .

───────── Eleven ─────────

THE SUPERIOR OFFICER must set the best example.

Trewley wasn't going to be caught out, least of all by Stone, the same way two days running. A late homeward departure and a heat-troubled sleep notwithstanding, next morning he was at his desk a full twenty minutes before the sergeant came hurrying in, heavy-eyed and full of apology.

"Never mind that." He waved her to his visitors' chair with a ferocious gesture of the report file he held in one hand. "You're here now—and you're not late. I'm early." He scowled. "I told you last night, after that fool interrupted us, we'd do better to go right through this lot with a decently clear head. Well—in principle, I have."

Stone looked hopeful. "And, sir?"

He subsided, sighing. "And you were right when you said we'd end up having to go round all of 'em in turn. There's not a damned thing stands out in any of this blasted bumf, beyond the odd question it'll take time to find answers for—like what does anyone know about this new headmistress before she came to Allingham? And what exactly are the financial arrangements of that Stitcherie affair with one partner dead? And—"

And the telephone rang on Trewley's paper-piled desk.

The superintendent, while acknowledging—with professed reluctance—the current mode for sexual equality, had tempered his language to a surprising degree since the advent of Sergeant Stone. He had perforce always kept a cool head at home, in deference to the presence of his wife and three daughters; he had bottled up his emotions to let them rip, when circumstances demanded, in comparative safety on his own male-populated ground. Legendary were some of the epithets hurled by the Plainclothes Prune at his quivering subordinates in moments of procedural stress; but Stone had been inclined to dismiss legend as exaggeration. . . .

Until, last night, some careless hand had slotted the wrong switchboard plug into the socket of the telephone extension to Trewley's office, and she realised that she had been very much mistaken.

She braced herself now for a repeat performance, as with an oath to blister paint the bulldog flung the reports aside, snatched up the receiver, and barked: "If I have to tell you idiots *again* I'm not to be disturbed except in an emergency—"

Whoever the idiot, he was both courageous and leather-lunged. From several feet away Stone could hear his desperate shout as he dared to break into the full flow of Trewley's infuriated eloquence. "Sir, listen—this *is* an emergency! There's been another murder!"

For a moment, silence. Trewley gaped at the receiver in his hand, took a deep breath, and jerked his head at Stone to listen in at her own desk. "Another murder," he repeated quietly once she was there. "Carry on, lad. Who is it?"

KATHLEEN SHOREY HAD gone to bed wondering whether she would ever sleep soundly again. The sad turmoil of previous terms—the new theatre building, the regrettable enforced retirement of poor Miss Waide, the appointment of an outsider to the post of headmistress—seemed now as nothing compared to the horrors of sudden, inexplicable death on St. Catherine's property, and the overwhelming incursion into the school's genteel privacy of the police with their exhaustive—and exhausting—questions.

A merciful, if slight, cooling of the night air just before

dawn at last allowed the deputy head to snatch an hour or two's relief from her mattress-tossing misery. She snatched in vain: the relief was minimal. Kathleen's eyes might sleep, but her brain could not. Across her dreaming vision whirled spectres of frightful clarity, their faces an incandescent green, their voices howls of glee above the wild accompaniment of an electric storm. A skeletal figure of stupendous size lashed out with a clattering arm to wrest a fork of lightning from the echoing sky. Bony fingers gripped, bony shoulders opened, eye-sockets flamed bloodred as the target was found; the arm swung up, and back; the lightning spear was poised—was aimed—was thrown—

"No!" Kathleen sat up with a shriek. She was hot: she was cold. Her sheet was on the floor, her pillows had been flung to the far side of the room. Her heart thumped in her chest; her forehead was damp; her breath came in gasps. She shuddered, struggling for self-control: it had been a dream, nothing more. The gibbering wraiths had no power to disturb her further, now that she was awake. . . .

The first shrill pipings of the dawn chorus, from a bird perched on the roof just above her window, made Kathleen leap from her bed and scuttle across the room almost in one movement. She fell against the door, gasping.

The jolt brought her back to her senses. "Disgraceful," she reproached herself as sternly as she could. "My nerves—to be worked up into such a state—so ridiculous, at my age, from one who is meant to set the girls a good example—yet I'm sure," she continued plaintively, "I won't sleep again tonight." As the bird sang again, her eyes turned automatically to the window. "This morning."

Morning. The day could begin. "I . . ." She licked her lips. "I shall wash, and dress, and have breakfast." Anything to restore, as far as possible in this changed world, the comforting sense of reality and routine. "Then I shall go to school. . . ."

Kathleen had supposed that she would be the first member of staff on the premises. She didn't count the janitor: in Kathleen's view, the only important people in the running of a school were the teachers. And few teachers— even those as dedicated as the St. Catherine's team—cared so much for the job that they would voluntarily go on duty at half-past five in the morning. It was therefore with a jolt, and the customary sinking flutter inside, that she recognised in the distance the tall form of Avis Thoday.

Miss Thoday was for once not wearing academic dress, but the absence of that long, black, flowing gown did little to alter her image as the bird of prey, of ill-omen, which she had assumed in Miss Shorey's eyes. The headmistress stalked with her measured, ominous tread along the corridor, around the corner, and out of sight, leaving the deputy it seemed she had not noticed quivering in silent distress against a shadowed section of the wall.

As soon as Miss Thoday was out of sight, Miss Shorey was herself again. She would not be deflected from her duty by more personal feeling. She would continue along the route she had previously mapped out . . . but would do so in the opposite direction, thus reducing the risk of bumping into her superior until the day was safely advanced to a more acceptable hour. She turned on her heel and set off with resolution in the direction from which Avis Thoday had just come.

She passed by the covered walkway from the old building to the new and found her feet taking her, as she'd known they would, to the door of the needlework room. All signs of the police presence had been removed (together with the infamous Burdena) late the previous afternoon. It had been decided that Friday's sewing classes would, like Thursday's, be cancelled, though as a mark of respect rather than from official necessity. The room itself would remain out of bounds until after the weekend.

Miss Thoday had also decreed that the tables, and those machines remaining, should be rearranged in such a way that the absence of the Burdena would be less conspicuous; and she had evinced some slight pique when the police—

who after all were moving everything in sight in order to check it—refused to oblige her in this. She then demonstrated far more sympathy to the needs of her own pupils than she'd shown to those of Gladys Franklin when, reminding the busy sleuths that public examinations were imminent, she had insisted that girls preparing for needlework exams must not be denied access to any essential equipment, this to be removed to the Old Building out of everyone's way once the police had finished with it. The police, bowing to superior moral forces, had accordingly removed.

Miss Shorey sighed as she contemplated the closed door of the needlework room. She knew that never—no matter how she might word a threat, petition, or command—would she be the equal of Avis Thoday for Getting Things Done. If she saw it as her Duty, Miss Thoday would never fail to carry it out—or (which was more in character) never fail to see that it was carried out by someone else. Someone over whom she had an authority legitimate as well as inherent . . .

Without thinking, Kathleen's hand moved to the knob of the locked door; she felt it chilly in her grasp, tingling against her fingers. Her fingers—she had no thought of using her master key—closed about the knob; her wrist and hand rotated automatically through ninety degrees.

There was a click, and the door opened.

The door opened, creaking inwards on its hinge, pulling Kathleen with it into the empty needlework room. . . .

Except that the room wasn't empty.

There was a crumpled form lying on the floor, shadowed in a corner of the room between two tables. . . .

Kathleen Shorey couldn't move. She stared, frozen to the spot, at the shadowy form in the corner—a form that, like Kathleen, did not move. Could not move.

For the first time in her life Miss Kathleen Dorothea Shorey succumbed to hysterics.

• • •

"I DON'T LIKE coincidence, Stone." Trewley gazed sorrow-fully down at the hapless female form on the floor of the needlework room. The deceased was—had been—a large, heavy woman of indeterminate years, with fair, faded hair seeming even more fair when contrasted with the puffy grey-blue of her face. "I don't hold with coincidence . . . not in a case like this, anyway." He rubbed his chin, and frowned. "Oh, I know in detective stories there's a second killer just waiting to take advantage of events to get rid of someone he doesn't like—but this is real life. I find it hard to credit there could be two murderers wandering around a place of this sort without somebody we haven't caught up with yet having spotted something a bit odd about one or other of the blighters." He brightened. "Or both. Give us time . . ."

"Or she, sir," said Stone, whom honesty compelled to strike this distasteful blow for women's liberation. "You said 'someone *he* doesn't like'—but it's not beyond the bounds of possibility that a woman could have done this."

"Could you?"

"I'm certainly strong enough." She knew he didn't refer to any moral scruples she might have. "But you wouldn't need judo to kill someone this way, if you took them by surprise." She contemplated his greater bulk and height, and had to smile. "Why, I could even kill you, sir, if you weren't paying proper attention."

"Careful," begged Trewley as his partner's hands came out of her pockets to demonstrate. In less solemn circum-stances he might have made some reference to the chances of her premature promotion; now he merely sighed and waited.

"If," said Stone, "I—he or she—came up behind you when you were sitting down, no problem. Not that I think that's what happened here. From the way she's lying, I'd say she was standing when he threw it round her neck—and it's certainly long enough to throw from a distance where he wouldn't need to get so close he'd put her on her guard."

"Or she," muttered Trewley, running an uneasy finger round the collar of his shirt. "Yes, I agree, she'll have been standing up, our lad was hovering around, not too near, nice and canny with that damned lasso in his hand, waiting for the right moment, and then . . . Ugh."

"But she was lucky, in a way. Normally," said Stone, trying to suppress her inevitable queasiness under the weight of an academic lecture, "it takes a good three minutes to asphyxiate someone of average health and fitness, which we'll assume for the moment she was. And it can be as long as a quarter of an hour." She made a face; Trewley grumbled under his breath. "It won't surprise me, though, if Doc Watson reports that she died almost immediately from, um, cerebral anaemia, or from vasovagal inhibition—that's a sort of shutting-down spasm of the heart, sir, which my guess would be is what happened here." Without using her repocketed hands, Stone contrived to indicate the neck and upturned face of the dead woman; Trewley bent to observe. "Despite the ligature around her neck, the usual indications of strangulation—petechial haemorrhages, cyanosed skin, and so on—aren't all that well developed, are they?"

The superintendent straightened, glanced at his subordinate, and nodded. "Could almost say she died of fright, I suppose," he ventured, and she did not disagree. He nodded again. "Too soon for him to finish what he'd planned to do the way he planned to do it—but he killed her, just the same."

"Oh, yes. But at least it was quick, poor thing. . . ."

There was a brief pause, during which they paid their silent respects to the woman lying dead before them; then they found themselves brushed aside by bearded Dr. Watson, a black-bagged whirlwind of exuberant energy in a hurry to make the pronouncement required of him by law so that he could return to his interrupted breakfast.

Trewley and Stone retreated to the corridor, leaving the needlework room, for the second time, to the tender mercies of the forensic team. Trewley ran another finger round his shirt collar, and grimaced.

"Nasty. Even nastier than the last one, quick or not. And I thought being electrocuted was bad enough. . . ."

"The last one was malice aforethought," Stone reminded him gently. "You don't just happen to swap two wires round by mistake—"

"And would you say it was all that likely anyone'd *just happen* to have the belt slip off a treadle sewing machine, nice and handy for wrapping round somebody's neck? There's forethought there, too, my girl." He rubbed his chin, gazing back into the shadowed corner where the body lay quietly at the hub of a bustling crowd, then averted his gaze to the opposite corner and the squat wooden shape that was the treadle sewing machine in its old oak casing.

"They made things to last in those days," Trewley said. "My mother had something similar: a lot of folk did. Lift up the lid and swing out the machine, get yourself a tabletop for spreading out the work. Lots of little drawers for pins and thread and the whatcher-call'ums, attachments; double doors back and front to get at the pedalling bit, and another door matching the drawers, for access to the drive wheels. And the drive belt—but the belt wouldn't last," he said slowly. "Rubber, that was, as I recall, and rubber perishes with time."

Stone said: "If you can use an old pair of tights for an emergency car fan belt . . ."

A pause. "You'd have thought she'd notice someone had been messing with the machine. . . ." Trewley rubbed his chin and brightened. "Of course, this corner's not immediately visible from the door. She would've walked right in without checking—keen to get a proper look at the site of the murder, I suppose. The first murder," he added grimly as Stone winced. "Or keen to get on with her work. It was her job to set the place straight after our lot had finished turning it upside down, according to Miss Thoday. . . ." The tone in which he delivered the final phrase would have won him no plaudits from the police Public Relations department. "What the hell do they expect? Of course fingerprint powder leaves a mark! And as for—"

"Yes, sir!" said Stone, watching him start to turn slowly purple, and worried for his blood pressure. "But about this belt—the plaited tights from the sewing machine, to be strictly accurate. Do you think there might be anything, um, significant in the choice of . . . of weapon?"

"It's not the most obvious method," he said, subsiding. "She was a big woman—but a man could've done it with his bare hands, if he caught her off guard. Could chummie be a woman? You said yourself, you could kill someone my size with a trick of that sort. And it doesn't need height or strength to switch two wires inside a floor control."

"I, um, was thinking more of a—a psychological clue, really." Stone hesitated. Her chief was seldom impressed by what he thought of as trick-cycling. "He couldn't know she would die so quickly, as we're supposing that she did. Strangling isn't a—a nice way of killing anyone, sir."

"For heaven's sake, Stone! I'm not a fool—"

"Not—not clean," she went on quickly. "Messy. You have to . . . be involved, with strangling. It isn't like swapping a couple of wires round and disappearing to the other end of the country, which he could easily have done for the first murder." Trewley grunted. "I just wondered why the two deaths were so very different in approach, sir. The only thing that links them seems to be the sewing theme, if we can call it that."

"They always return to the scene of the crime," Trewley reminded her. "Which happens to be the needlework room. So maybe she surprised him brooding about the place, and he had to do something about it, fast."

"Strangling may be . . . reliable, sir, but I'd hardly call it fast."

"It keeps the victim quiet, remember. No chance of her

yelling for help with her windpipe blocked—and, bearing
in mind what we were saying about malice aforethought, for
a spur-of-the-moment killing it's one of the best methods
there is." He snorted. "So we've got a choice. For all the
needles and pins and pairs of scissors there must be around
this place, he didn't stab the poor soul, he strangled her.
You're the medical expert, Stone. Did he kill her the way he
did as a spontaneous gesture—or was it some damned
symbolism for stopping her telling us what she knew?"

─────── Twelve ───────

WHILE MISS SHOREY'S left cheek wore a faint pinkish tinge, the rest of her face was sickly pale. Despite the cups of hot, sweet tea that had been poured into her by the Domestic Science mistress, Kathleen remained in a state of near collapse; only her overriding sense of duty gave her the strength to talk now to the police rather than suffering herself to be taken, wrapped in blankets, to Allingham General Hospital for observation.

"It was kind of you," Trewley began. "Very . . . courageous, Miss Shorey, agreeing to see us so soon after such a bad shock. But you understand, don't you, that it's very important we should find out exactly what happened this morning? And the sooner we do, the better chance we stand of catching the blighter before he does it again." *Or she,* he appended silently. The focus of police interest on the all-female St. Catherine's School was much sharper now than it had been after the first, more public, killing.

"Would you like to tell us in your own words how you came to find Mrs. French's body?" he went on as Kathleen preened herself on being dubbed courageous, and her previous look of dazed apathy became one of modest pride. The idea that the murderer might be disinclined to stop at two seemed to disturb her not in the slightest. "How about starting off," he prodded as she hesitated, "with why you were on the premises at . . ." The bloodhound did his best to twinkle. "At such an ungodly hour?"

If he'd hoped to startle her into a giveaway blush, he was disappointed. Kathleen did indeed turn pink, but with apparent embarrassment rather than from any guilty cause; and as she replied, her gaze was as steady as her voice.

Too steady? Trewley filed this thought away for future consideration as Kathleen began to speak.

"I couldn't sleep," she confessed. "Two nights running, such dreadful, dreadful dreams—as if that will come as any surprise to you, Superintendent—and it was so fearfully hot yesterday, as well. . . ."

Trewley nodded with every indication of complete sympathy with this point of view. Kathleen's awkward flush faded to a more becoming cream . . . apart from the marks on her left cheek. Stone gazed at these with some interest, yet said nothing as she applied herself to her notebook.

"Nobody," said Kathleen, "could call me a—a hysterical female." Trewley wondered whether anyone had in the past made such an accusation: another file-away thought. "But after what happened here on Wednesday, no reasonable person could blame anyone belonging to the school for being . . . upset." She sniffed. "And if the deputy head-mistress does not belong to a school, after so many years' loyal service, then I'm sure I don't know who does."

Trewley nodded again. Something in the emphasis she had placed on "deputy" and "so many years" caught his attention. "A newcomer can't possibly feel the same way," he agreed, his bulldog glower reduced to a kindly, brown-eyed beam. "It takes times to feel part of a place—to feel responsible, you might say."

"Indeed it does!" Kathleen sat bolt upright, her grey curls bouncing with the vigour of her assent. "One cannot—cannot assume responsibility merely by putting one's name to a piece of paper. *Authority*, yes—that is, authority can be so assigned—but mere . . . contractual obligation is not enough. One has to . . ." The blush returned, deeper than before. "One has to care," said Kathleen, and for the first time, her voice quivered. "As I care for dear St. Catherine's.

And such feelings—genuine feelings—do not grow overnight. And then, the longer they have been growing, the . . . the deeper they are. My—my whole life, I suppose, has been spent here."

"So you're a Katie?"

"I came here," said Miss Shorey, "as a preparatory pupil during the war. Away from the bombing . . ." She fell silent as she recalled the little girl of long ago, and her parents at vital work in the front line, resolved that, whatever might happen to them, their only child would have a better chance in life than they. She sighed. "It's thirty years since the Preparatory House had to be closed—the expense, you know. And for such young children to be away from home when there was no pressing danger seemed perhaps . . ."

Trewley nodded. "Not being rude, Miss Shorey, but you'd call yourself the oldest inhabitant, would you?"

"Most certainly I would. Which is why I feel—felt—feel," Kathleen recorrected herself, "responsible for what goes on here, in school hours or out of them. After Wednesday evening . . ." Once more she was pale, as recollection was more vivid than that of half a century before. "It was only to be expected that I would find it hard to relax that first night, but I was so sure I wouldn't be troubled the same way on Thursday that it came as a great surprise to me when I was. Such dreams . . . and I had the ridiculous notion that the school . . . needed me. Needed someone to watch over it—to care for it, in person—to prevent something even more terrible happening. . . ."

Her eyes, when she looked at Trewley, were bright with tears. "It wasn't so ridiculous after all, was it?"

"I'm afraid it wasn't, Miss Shorey."

He made himself sound just a little more bracing; and Kathleen was duly braced. "I arrived at around twenty to six, I suppose. It's a fifteen-minute walk from my house, and the milk hadn't come by the time I left, though I could hear the float somewhere nearby."

"Your milkman delivers at half past five?"

"He's very reliable. I can always trust him to pop the bottle under the saver—one of those earthenware coolers with a reservoir that evaporates—so it won't turn before I'm able to put it in the fridge. Sometimes, on Thursdays when he's late collecting money, I've left it all day with no bother, if I haven't gone back at lunchtime."

Trewley wondered what the local burglars made of this—presumably she left her money out with the empty bottles—then decided that catching a killer was more important than giving instructions on crime prevention. "You got here some time before quarter to six, let's say. What did you do then? Presumably you couldn't just walk into the place." He hoped. Crime prevention officer, where were you?

"I had intended," said Miss Shorey, once more with that strange emphasis, "to use my duplicate keys to enter the school, and then the staff room, to collect my master key from my locker. Mrs. Baxter—the bursar—has another set, of course, but I . . . We keep all the classrooms locked, you know, and of course after Wednesday we would have been . . ."

The anguished look that the superintendent turned upon his witness, clenched teeth notwithstanding, made her blink. Her left hand crept up to her cheek. Trewley struggled with his crime-prevention self—and won. He didn't say a word.

Miss Shorey pursed her lips. "Of course, once one has succeeded to a position of responsibility, one should lose no time in . . . living up to that responsibility. Which, to be fair"—it sounded a real effort for her to say the words—"I suppose Miss Thoday was trying to do. Yet someone who has only been half a term in the school cannot hope to be as familiar with the many customs, the rules and observances. . . . And if she had been doing anything like a thorough job," she finished, her eyes flashing, "how was it she never even saw poor Mrs. French?"

Any thoughts of a brief homily about Carelessness with

Keys vanished in the blinding light of a Significant Remark. Trewley sat up. "Are you saying Miss Thoday was there—on the premises—before you? But I'd understood . . ."

Once more Miss Shorey caressed her left cheek. "I spotted her in the distance as I arrived to find the main door unlocked. Naturally I was startled, and a little anxious—one thinks automatically of vandals, or burglars. I half wondered whether you—the police—might have had to come back to the school for some reason or other, and omitted to make all secure behind you, but . . . Of course," she added in haste as Trewley emitted a furious snort, "I knew that your training would never allow you to be so careless. I thought I might just take a quick look round to see if any harm had been done, and . . . I saw Miss Thoday."

"So," said Trewley, "no harm done. What was she doing?"

"Walking down the main corridor of the Old Building." Miss Shorey looked slightly uneasy. "I, ah, supposed that, like myself, she had been unable to sleep and was . . . on patrol, as one might call it."

"But you didn't join her. Two heads better than one, that sort of thing? Especially," Trewley said, "when there might have been vandals on the premises."

"Oh, once I saw Miss Thoday I realised there couldn't be. It was obvious that she was responsible for unlocking the door— and failing to lock it behind her. It was fortunate that it was I and not someone with less respect for the property of others who discovered the omission."

"In one way, yes." Trewley twinkled companionably at her. "Not so fortunate for you, though, was it? Coming across Mrs. French the way you did, first thing in the morning after a sleepless night."

With a sigh Miss Shorey concurred. Trewley was watching her closely, without seeming to do so. He said: "Now, I understand how you'd feel it'd be more efficient to check the place individually. Cover twice the area in the same time, and all that." He frowned. "What I can't understand is why, when if you saw her you must have been within hailing distance of Miss Thoday, you didn't at least compare notes with her about where she'd been, to save going over the same ground more than once."

He left it there. He didn't ask if it had been a simple case of her never thinking of such a move; he didn't ask if she doubted Miss Thoday's thoroughness; nor did he enquire whether the two of them had some quarrel that might render early-morning intercourse an awkwardness to be avoided. He left it there; he sat back, frowning as if in thought; and he waited.

St. Catherine's had always been a happy school. There was no place in the staff room or among the Governors for the cut and thrust of modern educational politics; jockeying for self-advancement was deemed offensive; wars of nerves were quite unknown. Kathleen Shorey, more than anyone else formed in the Katie mould, was not proof against the tactics of Superintendent Trewley. After hesitation for only a few moments, she made her confession.

In a way it would be wonderful to be able, for once, to speak her mind freely. "I . . . don't greatly care for Miss Thoday," she said. "I certainly would not from choice associate with her any more than—than I must—and in this instance I did not think that such association was essential. Once I realised that her carelessness had caused her to leave the door open, I . . . I hoped she would not see me. And she didn't."

"In a corridor?" Straight, narrow, nowhere to hide . . . "Dark, was it?"

"The lights weren't on, this is true, but there are panels of frosted glass set at intervals along the wall of each class-room, level with the external windows. Pupils in class aren't distracted by anyone passing in the corridors, yet enough natural light filters through from outside to render the use of electricity almost unnecessary during the day." Miss Shorey sounded as gratified by this economy as if she had thought of it herself. "It was an improvement carried out at the behest of Miss Waide's predecessor, who had the alterations made during the Easter holiday of 1939. She was a woman of quite remarkable foresight and political awareness."

There was a short pause, during which silent tribute was paid to the memory of the six grim years that had followed the momentous events of 1939. Then Trewley said:

"So, light—but with enough patches of shadow to know she wouldn't see you if you kept still. Which you did. And off she went . . . and so did you. Why did you go in that particular direction?"

"Because it was the direction from which Miss Thoday had just come." Kathleen's eyes gleamed faintly. "It occurred to me that there was far less risk of our paths crossing if she were in the Old Building and I in the new. If I traced what I believed to be her path in reverse . . ."

"Umph." There was another pause. "It was Miss Thoday who raised the alarm after you'd made the discovery, they tell me. Why?"

Miss Shorey knew very well what he meant. "Why was it not I?" Her face flamed; her eyes fell; her hand crept to her cheek. "I am afraid that I . . . made a scene." If she was going to tell the truth . . . "Disgraced myself. Never before have I been so . . ." She gulped. "But—on top of everything else, to find . . ."

Trewley rubbed his chin, his gaze unfocused as he tried to envisage the general layout of the school. Stone, watching Kathleen as she began to shiver, made a movement that at last succeeded in turning that gaze in her direction.

Gently she shook her head. The superintendent's mouth twisted to one side; his eyes asked a silent question. The sergeant shook her head again as Kathleen Shorey, fumbling blindly in her pocket for a handkerchief, withdrew it with shaking hands. She dabbed helplessly at her tears, and her breath began coming in tremulous gasps.

The superintendent sighed. "You've been most helpful, Miss Shorey, but you've had enough for now, haven't you?

Thank you for all your help. We'll leave you in peace—for a while." It was the shortest of pauses. Only a keen ear—or a guilty conscience—would have noticed it. Stone heard it clearly: did Kathleen Shorey, too?

"We can supply the rest, I think," Trewley told his subordinate as they abandoned Miss Shorey to the renewed ministrations of the Domestic Science mistress, and headed for a more private location. "She opens the door, sees the body, throws a considerable wobbly . . . and along comes that bossy headmistress to box the poor woman's ears. Probably been waiting weeks for the chance, and couldn't believe her luck when it came."

"I suspect the feeling is mutual, sir."

"You're female, Stone." She suppressed the obvious retort. "Would you say it was a—a personality thing, or does it go deeper? Petty women's squabbles, or . . . ?"

"Or professional jealousy?" Stone considered the point dispassionately. "Mostly the latter, I'd say, with a touch of inferiority complex on top. Miss Thoday won the plum job—a job Miss Shorey, in the circumstances, might have had good reason to suppose would be given to her. It's understandable there would be a certain amount of . . . friction."

"We'll have a better idea once we've talked to Thoday," Trewley said. "But it's a funny thing, Stone. Here's the two of 'em, obviously at loggerheads in the most discreet sort of way—places like this don't go in for knock-down drag-out fights—yet all the time we're chatting to her, Shorey misses out on her chance to stir up trouble for the other one by asking the question that would get us wondering a good deal more about Thoday than we seem to have done so far. Granted she was raising the roof with her hysterics—hear her for miles, most likely, the way these corridors echo— and of course we've no idea how long she was yelling before Thoday heard her.

"But how come she heard her? What was Thoday doing

in the New Block? According to Shorey, who's no great friend, she'd been there once already. Why go back?"

"Er . . . Guilty conscience." It was Stone's job, as the loyal sidekick, to act as a sounding-board and supply random suggestions. At this stage in a murder enquiry, one theory was as good as another, so long as it encouraged the process of ratiocination. "She'd found the body on her tour of duty and didn't want to draw attention to herself by being the acknowledged first on the scene: everyone knows the one who finds the body is automatically suspect. When Miss Shorey saw her leaving the scene of the crime, she was going off somewhere to work out what to do next . . . and she did. Work it out, I mean. She decided to hang about in the general vicinity—nobody's going to ask a headmistress what she's doing anywhere on school premises—until someone came along and gave her a legitimate reason to . . . to have left the traces of her earlier presence our forensic tests were bound to show up."

"Umph. All right, as far as it goes. I was thinking the same myself. . . . But guilty conscience because she's the murderer, or for some other reason?"

Stone considered Avis Thoday as a double killer. It was possible. Anything was possible, she had found, with human nature. Or . . . "Or she has Secrets, sir. She's a newcomer to Allingham. She'd assume we'd want to find out more about her—and there's something in her past life of which she feels ashamed, to say the least." She snapped her fingers. "Of course! She has some hold over someone who helped her obtain the position as headmistress, but it works both ways. If anyone found out . . ."

"Cleaning ladies empty wastepaper baskets," Trewley said. "They find scribbled notes, and envelopes with hand-writing they might recognise. . . . Oh, yes, it's quite possible that Brenda French found out something the killer didn't want anyone else to know. . . .

"But how the devil did Lois Tanner find it, too?"

Thirteen

THE TWO DETECTIVES found Miss Thoday in her study, at her desk, with an empty coffee cup to one side of the blotter. She was talking on the telephone and did not appear in the least startled by their arrival. She motioned them calmly to be seated as she finished her conversation, and continued making notes on a large sheet of paper ruled in columns and closely written, but scribbled over with cryptic arrows, balloons, and similar pencilled symbols suggestive of last-minute alterations to some complex plan.

". . . taken into consideration," she concluded. "Unfortunate as these circumstances are, the girls are not to be penalised for something that is entirely beyond their control. A meeting with the Public Examination Board must be arranged at the earliest possible moment. . . ."

Trewley and Stone gathered that Miss Thoday, while willing to accept the necessary closure of part of her school and the homeward dismissal of half her pupils for the second time in a week, was once more disposing that such pupils as had state exams to sit should sit them, police activity notwithstanding. The perfect headmistress. Or—was she?

"Superintendent," said Miss Thoday with an apologetic smile as she settled the receiver back on its cradle. "And Sergeant," she added punctiliously, the smile more impersonal towards a junior. "I regret keeping you waiting, but I am sure you will appreciate that I, like yourselves, have had a good many matters under consideration this morning."

"You certainly have." Trewley nodded, one busy professional to another. "There won't be too much of a problem with the exams, will there? Rough luck on the girls if they get marked down because of all the upset."

Miss Thoday raised elegant eyebrows at this meiosis. "The examiners and the County Education Officer are being kept fully informed. There should be little difficulty in convincing them that the results from St. Catherine's should be judged by slightly different standards than those from other schools." From the look on her face and the tone of her voice, it was evident that such difficulties as there might have been were now of no importance.

"It is, however, the nonexamination pupils who pose more of a problem," she went on, indicating the ruled and overwritten sheet on her desk. "They can only be sent home for a limited period without falling dangerously far behind in their studies. While so many of the rooms in the New Block must remain out of service—for what I trust, Superintendent, will not be too long a period—I have contrived some emergency measures that I believe will serve." She uttered this belief without a hint of doubt. "Subject to your permission, desks from classrooms near the needlework room will be removed to the gymnasium: the janitor and a group of workmen are already covering the floor with rolls of felt carpet I have borrowed from the Town Council . . . on indefinite loan." A faint sigh escaped her. "In my opinion, one should always hope for the best, but prepare for the worst."

"And take what comes," supplied Trewley as Miss Thoday regarded him with a thin, quizzical smile.

"Quite so, Superintendent. Should the worst occur, we also have the new theatre." Merciful heaven, how many more murders did the woman expect? "The seats in the auditorium are, admittedly, fixed to the floor, but they were designed to be removed if necessary. Scenery flats could be used as screens to divide one group of desks from another, but since it is far simpler to convert the gymnasium than the theatre to classroom use, that is what will be done."

Trewley wasn't one for foreign languages, and couldn't be sure of how it was pronounced, but he thought *sang froid* the understatement of the century to describe the reaction of Avis Thoday to two brutal killings on school property in the first term of her headship. Efficiency was one thing, but this cold-blooded super-detachment made him squirm.

It also made him wonder. Anyone as callous as it seemed Miss Thoday was might be capable of anything. Anything . . . She must be an intelligent woman. Fools didn't snatch prestigious headships from under the noses of more deserving rivals. But wouldn't an intelligent woman realise how badly it must look if she didn't show a little more emotion over what had happened? Miss Shorey had gone into shock, while Miss Thoday, by her own account, had merely boxed her deputy's ears, brought her to her senses, and gone off to phone for help without turning a hair. Intelligence would surely try to avoid suspicion by staging just a brief scene. . . . But would a super-intelligence not bother, super-confident that there was no need because the plodding police would never discover the truth. . . .

Trewley almost enjoyed dealing with super-confident crooks. Sooner or later they overreached themselves and made a mistake. All he hoped was that it wouldn't take the third murder Miss Thoday had already portended before whatever mistake it was going to be had been made. . . .

"Superintendent?" His super-cool suspect was regarding him with a look of unruffled curiosity. He felt like a specimen on a dissecting slab, and could imagine he saw the gleam of sharpened steel reflected in her eyes. "I must apologise, Superintendent, if I have interrupted some vital train of thought, but I had rather the feeling that it was more a trance brought on by sheer boredom at my over-lengthy exposition on the complexities of the school timetable." Miss Thoday achieved a smile. "I apologise again for

having taken up so much of your valuable time with these
unimportant matters—relatively unimportant, that is, though
to the young ladies concerned perhaps not. You came to ask
me questions, however, and to take a statement. Feel free to
ask, and to take, as you will."

In the event, once Trewley had pulled himself together,
she had little at first to add to what he and Stone already
knew, or had guessed. She justified her presence at the
school at so early an hour by claiming, as Kathleen Shorey
had claimed, a sleepless night and a not unnatural anxiety
for the future, induced by memories of the recent past. She
had not noticed Miss Shorey's arrival at the school; she
attributed her failure to relock the main door to the
afore-said anxiety; she was, being tall, a quick walker, and
had come when she did to the rescue of the distraught Miss
Shorey by sheer happenstance, being midway through her
second tour of duty round the buildings old and new. . . .

"So you'd been past the needlework room once already."
Trewley frowned. "Why didn't you notice the first time that
something was wrong?"

Only now did a hint of unease become apparent in the
demeanour of Miss Thoday. "It must sound . . . foolish,
Superintendent, when my express purpose for being on the
premises was to ascertain that all was well, but . . . the door
of the needlework room was the only one in the entire
school I somehow . . . did not care to check." She coughed.
"A most regrettable weakness on my part. I am not normally
given to superstitious hysteria, believe me." He believed
her. "But on this particular occasion . . ."

"It's not so surprising," said Trewley. "Unusual circumstances breed unusual responses. I shouldn't think you can
have been in this sort of situation before—not unless they
went in for bumping each other off at your old school, of
course. I take it they didn't."

The arch of Miss Thoday's outraged eyebrows made
them almost invisible beneath her stylish coiffeur. "The
Bishop of Stortford Foundation," she informed the superin-

tendent coldly, "is one hundred and forty-seven years old. In that century and a half there has been not one incident that has merited the least breath of scandal. Nor am I prepared to accept," she said even more coldly, "until the full facts are known, that there need be any . . . imputation against the staff or pupils of St. Catherine's." She favoured the two detectives with a withering look. "Until the full facts are known," she repeated, icicles in every syllable. "Which is the responsibility of you and your colleague, Superintendent, as the continued smooth running of St. Catherine's is mine. If there are no further questions, might I suggest that we each pursue our respective tasks with the greatest possible expedition?"

Trewley could never explain how it happened that, fifty seconds after this proposal had been made, he and Stone were outside Miss Thoday's study, closing the door, while she remained seated at her desk. Even before they had reached the door, she was back at work on the time-table. . . .

His sergeant couldn't explain it, either.

"Talk about a monstrous regiment of women!" The polka-dot handkerchief was proving its worth as it had seldom done before. "Box poor old Shorey's ears? I'm amazed the blasted female didn't—didn't bite her head clean off!"

This was not the place for a lecture on the true meaning of John Knox's oft-misquoted words. Stone said mildly: "She knows we can check it out, of course. Do you think she was banking on our thinking just that, and not bothering?"

"Umph." Trewley replaced the handkerchief, shrugged his shoulders, and considered the question. "The Stortford Foundation—that's over in Loamshire somewhere, isn't it?"

"Near the coast." Stone made a face. "Sea breezes, a bracing climate, and compulsory team games until your final year. Ghastly."

"She doesn't much look the outdoor type. Can't see that

hairdo and those clothes charging up and down a muddy hockey field blowing whistles in all directions, can you?"

"Maybe that's why she came here, sir."

Trewley stopped and looked at her. "Now then, Detective Sergeant Stone, use your brains." Only when he thought he had scored did he ever address her by her full title. "You don't land this sort of job without having worked your way up through the ranks. The blighters expect you to have had the complete experience so you can tell everyone else how to do it once you're the one in charge. And there's no denying she's a bossy woman, Stone."

"No, sir." Stone hid a smile. "But perhaps, with due respect, sir"—his full title was an impertinence the sergeant would never dare—"she served her, um, subaltern period somewhere else. Perhaps the Foundation wasn't her first school." She sounded as if she knew what she was talking about. "Stortford's every bit as classy as St. Catherine's, sir. They don't take beginners. She could have been safely past the hockey-whistle stage by the time she came to Loamshire."

Trewley looked at her again. The brown eyes smouldered for a moment in the corrugated face; then he chuckled, clapped her on the shoulder, and strode off down the corridor without another word. Stone pattered in his wake, no longer concealing her amusement.

At the main door he stopped. "If you're wrong," he said, "and she wasn't—safely past, I mean—or if it *was* her first school . . . then it just goes to show what a damn good actress the woman must be. Which comes as no great surprise, Stone."

"We'll have to check."

"We're going to be busy little bees, all right." He scowled through the side window at the shimmer of air rising from sunbaked flagstones in the courtyard. He was more than reluctant to leave the relative coolness of high-vaulted corridors to confront the sultry torment of the outside world:

but it had to be done. Though perhaps not quite yet. "With being Saturday tomorrow . . ."

"If we radio a message through now, sir, someone from Loamshire might get on to it before the weekend starts, with any luck."

The bulldog snarled something about luck which had Stone in discreet convulsions, though she soon recovered.

"We'll radio now," she said again, and slipped past him to open the door. Sighing, muttering once more of bossy woman, the superintendent trudged in his sergeant's wake down the front steps, and across to where the police car was parked on the very edge of the last patch of shadow.

Professional courtesy required that she make the offer. "Would you care to do the honours, sir?" She hoped very much that he wouldn't. While esteeming her superior's many fine qualities, she had to admit there were one or two weaknesses that could prove, on occasion, inconvenient. Or worse. His complete inability to cope with anything of a mechanical nature meant that the car radio, more often than not, was out of commission. Why it should be so difficult for him to grasp the principle of pushing one small switch gently to the left, she had never been able to decide. . . .

"Carry on, Sergeant." He didn't smile: he was already wilting with the heat, his handkerchief mopping his clammy brow as the bloodhound eyes looked sunken in the lugubrious face. "Make it snappy. I can't stand too much of this."

The misanthropic voice at the answering end of the radio waves was its usual accommodating self. Didn't Sergeant Stone realise it was Friday? Stone assured the Voice that both she and Superintendent Trewley were well aware of this fact. Were they also aware that Friday was market day in Stortford? Warily Stone confessed their mutual ignorance.

"Oh, my God!" broke from Trewley as light dawned. From the loudspeaker came a sharp intake of breath.

"Blasphemy," the Voice informed the superintendent in

tones of hellfire doom, "is anathema. Moreover, it should be unnecessary as a form of self-expression for those who are supposed," the Voice added with pointed emphasis, "to set an example. It is also illegal to pollute the airwaves with—"

Trewley polluted them again, crisply and at high volume. The Voice, muttering, subsided. It refused to make promises, saying merely that the superintendent's message would be passed to the appropriate Loamshire authorities as soon as possible—the clear inference being that possibilities were distinctly limited at that particular time. Once (conceded the Voice, very grudgingly) there was anything to report, it would be reported.

The connection was broken with a vicious click. Trewley and Stone regarded each other for a moment in silence. It was Stone who eventually broke it.

"I wish you wouldn't, sir. You know how it always gets you going—and in weather like this, with blood pressure like yours . . ."

"Market day!" he growled. "It would be. Everyone and his wife in town. Twice the volume of traffic. Lorries unloading and blocking the roads, stalls collapsing, cars double-parked, and the wardens having to be rescued from punch-ups by coppers who ought to be out and about cooperating on honest police work for their colleagues. Fly-by-night barrow-boys being hauled in under the Trades Descriptions Act, honest citizens taking the law into their own hands and getting arrested . . ."

The plaintive litany came to a halt as the superintendent ran out of anguished breath. Stone rushed in where lesser mortals might have hesitated.

"It could be worse, sir. At least it won't be *us* fighting our way through all the kerfuffle to talk to whoever's in charge at the school . . . and even if we don't find out until Monday—well, Miss Thoday is only one line of investigation, after all. We've a list of suspects—witnesses—as long as your arm. Someone, somewhere, is bound to know something: it's just a matter of asking the right questions. Who shall we talk to next?"

But Trewley was sunk in gloom, and for a long minute could not bring himself to reply.

── Fourteen ──

WHILE BENSON, HEDGES, and other members of his team carried out most of the routine interviews, Trewley elected to talk to the employer of the late Brenda French.

This was not as simple as it had at first seemed. He had automatically supposed the cleaning lady to have been the employee, and thus in death the responsibility, of the St. Catherine's board. Mrs. Baxter, the Katies' dragon bursar, soon enlightened him. Unlike the janitor, living with his wife and family in a tied cottage in a corner of the school grounds, Brenda French had worked for, and been paid by, Allingham Town Council, who (as it were) leased her services courtesy of assorted grants from the County Education Board and then (as one might say) subcontracted them out again to a number of educational establishments in and around the town.

"She didn't just clean this place, then?"

Mrs. Baxter was cautious in her reply. "I would hardly care to say one way or the other, Superintendent. I merely felt that you should be alert to the possibility—given the financial restrictions under which the council has been placed in recent years—that she might not have done. In the interests of economy, the council—her employers—have been forced to adopt an approach of more . . . flexible efficiency, if you understand me. The school itself has no authority over the, ah, working whereabouts of Mrs. French, and, provided that an appropriate number of cleaners clean the premises to the required standard, we have no particular interest in the administrative details, either. We certainly keep no records as to which cleaner does the cleaning on any given day."

"Well, I can see they'd find it difficult to . . . to clock on, like a factory, in a school. But are you saying you've got absolutely no way of knowing how many of 'em are here, and who works where, and when?"

"Why," countered Mrs. Baxter, "should we need to? If the cleaning is carried out to our satisfaction, what is the sense in generating extra paperwork, when it would only duplicate information already held by the council?"

This point had not occurred to him. "Of course," he was forced to agree: he disliked bumf as much as the next man—or woman. There was even the hint of a twinkle in the bulldog's eye, before sudden realisation dawned. "You mean the cleaners just . . . turn up when they please, and go home when they want? This whole place is left wide open until everyone's finished—and nobody knows when that is, because nobody has to tell anybody else that they have?"

Mrs. Baxter blinked. He had seemed almost friendly, for a moment, before turning so . . . accusing. "There are timesheets," she said defensively. "And at the end of the shift the head cleaner collects all the keys and returns them to the hook in my office. Then she locks my door and—"

The bloodhound smothered a howl. "*All the keys?* How many sets are there, for God's sake? No—don't tell me," he said as Mrs. Baxter looked decidedly alarmed. "More than enough." Crime prevention? These idiots didn't know the meaning of the words. "Enough for anyone who likes to pop into town any evening to that late-night shoe place and have another spare cut—a dozen of the damn things, if they want—and still be back in time to empty the wastepaper baskets and dust the odd desk and shove a mop over the floor and get her name ticked off for a job well done." He closed his eyes and groaned. "And the gaffer locks your office with her own spare key—and slips yours under the mat all nice and tidy for tomorrow morning, right?"

With a blush, Mrs. Baxter had to admit that, broadly speaking, the superintendent had guessed the truth.

This advice did not appear to gratify him. From the way he was gritting his teeth, it was clear he could bear it no longer. Stone, taking notes, wondered if a warning cough would remind him of his blood pressure or be regarded as insubordination. While she was making up her mind, Trewley continued.

"We need to talk," he barked, "to whoever might know just what has been going on around here. Who's the boss of the mop-and-duster brigade at the council?"

Mrs. Baxter blushed still more. She hesitated. Trewley opened his mouth to bark again. "Miss Broome!" she confessed in a tone that implied she knew she would not be believed.

She was correct. The superintendent's brows met in an awful frown. "Miss Broome," he repeated grimly. "Mrs. Baxter, this is no time for—"

"No, really! She jokes about it herself, sometimes—says it was foreordained. Her job, I mean. She's officially the Head of Domestic Services. Miss . . . Heather Broome."

Trewley took a deep breath; the bloodhound jowls quivered. He exhaled. "Thank you very much, Mrs. Baxter. We may be back later. Come along, Sergeant."

Outside in the flagstoned yard, the air wasn't so much shimmering as boiling. The sun blazed with tyrant beams from an implacably cloudless sky, keeping saviour breezes in distant, desperate exile. Crossing to the car felt like walking, face-deep in syrup, through a furnace.

The metal handles of the doors were untouchable. Trewley wrapped his red silk polka-dots around his hand; Stone, who for reasons of hygiene preferred disposable paper, deftly hitched up the hem of her wide split skirt. Blowing on their tingling fingers, the two detectives buckled themselves into their seat belts.

"The council offices, sir?" Stone glanced cautiously at her companion. "Or, um, should I just slip back and leave a message for one of the others to check the key cutters? We don't want to bother with something as routine as that, when it's all so chaotic anyway."

"You're a good girl, Stone. Women! Talk about handing it to burglars on a plate . . ."

"Yes, but they haven't been burgled, have they?" Then she had to giggle at how ludicrous it sounded. As if murder—double murder—weren't a thousand times worse than any mere break-and-enter-with-intent. "Unless the killer was interrupted, of course. Twice." She shook her dark head, thinking aloud. "Only . . . if I were going to pinch anything from a school, it would be the electrical teaching stuff—video recorders, projectors, taping equipment from the language lab, computers . . . I wouldn't have thought there'd be much of a market for back-of-a-lorry sewing machines, would you?"

"Stone, you've been educated, which means you're meant to have brains—which, compared to some of the moronic tea leaves we've got in these parts, you have. Use them, girl. You've seen the tuppenny-ha'penny locks on those doors—" He broke off, still fuming at the cavalier approach to crime prevention practised by the staff of St. Catherine's School. "Education be damned! Brains don't mean common sense, Stone—but at least," he said with a sigh, "they had sense enough to add an extra lock to the rooms with the teaching stuff in, even if . . . but they did add them." Another sigh. "They *look* impressive. You know the idle devil your average burglar is. He likes to play it cool. Doesn't want a lot of work—or a lot of noise. What tea leaf, especially in weather like this, is going to bash his way through twice as much work as he needs?"

"Once, sir, I accept. Yes. But why go back a second time? Even a stupid thief must realise that's asking for trouble. What on earth can be in the needlework room to make it worth killing for—twice?"

"'S what we're paid to find out." He slumped in his seat, fanning himself with the handkerchief he hadn't yet replaced in his pocket. "Oh, forget the key cutting for a while: I need some air. Let's get along to the town hall. We can call a message in while we're on the road."

Stone sent up a silent prayer on behalf of her radio, mentally booking it, yet again, into the repair shop; then she turned the keys, gunned the engine, and drove the police car away from St. Catherine's with the windows as far down as they would go.

Allingham defied modern taste in being proud of its town hall, a Victorian Gothic pile constructed of brick, faced with sandstone ashlar. The natives did not mock, they merely smiled at the way the architect had so obviously overdosed on Arthurian splendours when he drew up the design. The building had massive wooden doors both internal and external, darkly leaded diamond-pane windows, oak beams in every room, and a great number of turrets, reached by spiral stairs about which the Health and Safety people were always complaining.

Trewley and Stone voiced a few complaints of their own when Miss Broome agreed to see them at once in her office, and they learned there was no lift.

"The exercise will do us good, sir." Stone, philosophically accepting the situation, had already resolved to suffer a tactful shortness of breath halfway through the climb. "Better not rush it, though."

"If it's the heat you're fussing about, compared to outside this place is a refrigerator." Trewley didn't shiver, but for the first time in some hours he wasn't groping automatically for his handkerchief. "What must it be like in winter?"

"The human body," Stone informed her superior as they began their upward path, "takes longer to adjust to temperature change than most people realise; and when it does, it takes as long to adjust back again, no matter what the temperature's like now. In winter, for example, unless you're wrapped up really well against the cold, your blood will thicken, and you run the risk of clots—that's why it's so daft for just one or two people to push a car out of a snowdrift. The extra effort involved—"

"Talking of effort . . ." Trewley stopped, panting, to lean against a pillar. "Oof. Wonder how Miss Broome likes this damn safari every day."

From the look of the lady when they finally reached her office, Miss Broome could have had few strong objections to her regular spells of mountaineering. She was a thin, wiry, spry-looking individual of middle years, with a decided air of competence about her which showed that, had she chosen to object, there would have been an immediate alteration in her office arrangements.

"Exercise is good for me," she told Trewley and Stone once the latter, granting her superior a few minutes longer to catch his breath, had completed the official introductions and asked the inevitable question. "Besides, there's the view. On a clear day you can see for miles."

But not today: one mile would be stretching it. The whole of Allingham had been wrapped by a smothering solar hand in a hazy grey-blue blanket of photochemical gauze that grew ever thicker towards the outskirts of the town, and became almost opaque as town gave way to countryside. Stone shuddered. At ground level one didn't always realise just what was going on.

"Yes, well, you didn't come all this way to admire the scenery." Miss Broome sat herself at her desk, and her eyes lost their sparkle. "Brenda French—a dreadful business. One of our most reliable workers, on the list for years. Of course, with her husband a drunk, poor thing, she had no real chance to be anything else. Work means money, money means you keep a roof over your head and see your children decently clothed and properly fed, and if your husband won't do it, then it's up to you."

Trewley looked shaken. "Good Lord, if there's a husband, we really should've talked to him first. Not being rude, Miss Broome, but in most cases we prefer to let the immediate family know before outsiders, even people from work. We had no idea the poor woman was married. The school seemed to know nothing about her at all."

"I'm not surprised. Brenda could gossip with the best—with bells on!—but she wouldn't have had much in common about which to gossip with any of the Katie crowd even if she'd run across them, which in the usual way she wouldn't. School cleaners don't tend to arrive on the premises until most people have gone home—not that they're moonlighting, you understand, but so many of them work at other places first." Trewley and Stone sat up.

"Factories," said Miss Broome, "working shifts. Council offices, of course. Private functions on public premises—that's why we keep such detailed records of who's working where, and when. We couldn't possibly keep track of the money otherwise—which reminds me," she added as her visitors quietly digested this information. "Brenda's husband drank himself to death four years ago, and the children have long since left home. You needn't worry about . . . breaches of etiquette, Superintendent."

"That her file?" Trewley nodded thanks for the reassurance, then switched his attention to the pale green folder on Miss Broome's desk. "Can you tell us the other places she worked over, say, the past couple of weeks?"

Miss Broome sighed. "I wondered if this was the type of thing you might wish to know, and I've already checked. There's a tragic irony in what's happened, Superintendent." She sighed again. "Mrs. French hadn't worked anywhere. You see, she was not only overweight, but severely asthmatic as well. She took great care not to work where there were too many chemicals, which made the asthma worse. . . ."

Stone's head had gone up at the mention of a medical condition, and Miss Broome turned courteously towards her. "You have a question, Sergeant?"

"Um—not yet, thank you. Please go on, Miss Broome. You might answer it before I need to ask it."

Miss Broome nodded. "As I said, airborne chemicals

made Brenda's asthma much worse: she had to sign off sick almost a month ago. You must be aware of how poor the air quality has been in recent weeks." Trewley in particular was very well aware. "So many places use chemicals nowadays that they cannot be avoided completely—every office, for example, has a photocopier—but in normal circumstances it never seemed to cause too much of a problem, and in a school there are fewer than in, say, a factory. With the dreadful weather, though, poor Brenda found that even places where she'd been able to work before were simply . . . impossible."

"She must have been bad," said Stone sympathetically. Current regimens for the treatment of asthma involved daily inhalation of corticosteroids, with use of the more powerful bronchodilators saved for emergencies. With some prudent juggling, and top-ups where necessary, most asthmatics could lead a normal life. "Poor thing . . ."

"Poor indeed. She had her sick pay, of course, but . . ." Miss Broome leaned forward and lowered her voice. "I do hope this won't cause trouble for her family, when you find them—unpaid tax, you know—but . . . Well, you see, we were her only *legitimate* employers. Not that we encouraged her to—to defraud the government, please don't think that, and of course I never knew this officially, but I fear that the black economy had one of its most enthusiastic supporters in Brenda French."

"Not surprising," said Trewley to the surprise of Sergeant Stone. The superintendent was usually the first to condemn any infringement of the law. "With her husband on the booze, she'd want cash in hand so all she'd have to show him would be the council pay-slips. Save the rest to give the kids a decent start in life. . . ."

Miss Broome ventured a smile. "Thank you, Mr. Trewley. That's just how it was—except, of course, that with her husband's death and the children's adult departure, there was no need for her to carry on with the . . . subterfuge. She could have regularised the situation and saved herself a

good deal of worry . . . but I believe she had rather
developed a taste for living dangerously. Cocking a snook at
authority, perhaps—and nobody, after all, likes paying tax."

"How they finally got Al Capone," muttered Trewley,
who sometimes came out with the oddest snippets of
information.

Miss Broome looked startled, but otherwise ignored the
remark. "You can imagine that Brenda was keen to return to
work—any work—as soon as she could. She ended up in
hospital at one point, but I gather they gave her rather a
talking-to about her drugs, and sensible management, and so
on. And when she turned up Monday and said she was able
to start work at once, I . . ." Her face twisted in dismay. "I
believed her. That's the tragedy of it, Superintendent. If I
hadn't believed her, of course I wouldn't have let her go
back to St. Catherine's. And if she hadn't gone back to St.
Catherine's, poor Brenda French might still be alive. . . ."

——————— Fifteen ———————

Friday, Saturday, Sunday. Interviews, statements, photographs, reports. Paperwork by what felt like the ream, and probably was. Postmortem results, timesheets, flowcharts, and tables of opportunity; aching heads, tense shoulders, and tired eyes as people sat for hours at their desks checking, double-checking, analysing . . .

After the weekend things grew worse as the mercury hit ninety for the eighth day running. A journalist from the *Allingham Argus*, desperate for a scoop, fried an egg on the bonnet of the mayor's official limousine in the car park at the town hall; a traffic warden who remonstrated with the heat-maddened reporter had the remaining five eggs forcibly scrambled in her hair; and a security guard, rushing to the rescue, broke his leg on melting lard. The Casualty Department at Allingham General went to red alert as asphalt liquefied on the new stretch of motorway, and a juggernaut, trapped in pungent black treacle, jackknifed across all three carriageways and caused a multiple pileup.

"Good news, sir!" Detective Sergeant Stone danced into the office, smiling broadly.

The jaded bloodhound slumped on Trewley's chair dragged himself out of his blissful North Pole daydream back to brutal reality. "Somebody's confessed?"

"Er . . . no. But," she said, setting a welcome tray of tea and buns on the superintendent's blotter, "I slipped outside for—joke—a breath of air on the way back from the canteen . . . and I saw clouds on the horizon!"

"Rain?" The brown eyes gleamed. If true, this was the best news he'd had for a month.

"My bet is, yes." Her smile wavered as she addressed herself to her mug. "They did look an awful lot like thunderclouds—but," she added bravely, "if it means this weather's going to break at last, I don't think I care." She sipped her tea again. "Well, not very much."

"Pleate's bound to have a ghetto-blaster in that damned cupboard of his." Trewley munched a mouthful of bun with an air of real enjoyment. "If we could listen to the forecast on local radio, at least we'd know one way or—"

"No, sir." Stone held her superior with a glittering eye. "Not me. Not after last time—though if *you* fancy a spot of honest burglary, I don't mind keeping cave for you." She grinned wickedly. "I'll lend you my penknife, and—"

"Thanks, but no thanks." The bun now tasted stale in his mouth. "Like you said, not after last time. Is there anyone there we could ring?"

She knew what he meant. "They have a weather hotline, though I forget the number. But I believe it *is* going to break, sir. Doesn't your head feel . . . funny?" She rubbed gently at her temples. "Throbbing. Tight. As if somebody had wrapped a stocking round and was pulling it tighter and tighter all the time. . . ."

"Or the belt from a treadle sewing machine," he reminded her grimly. "Never mind the weather breaking—what about the case? Both of 'em," he added. "For all the sense we've made of what we've learned so far, it might just as well still be Wednesday evening. Five whole days, Stone, and two murders. Where the hell are we going wrong?"

"We could go over the evidence again," she began, then caught his eye and subsided. She understood as well as he did the Law of Diminishing Returns. "We could . . . we could check out the Bishop of Stortford Foundation for ourselves, instead of relying on what we've been told."

Running a wistful finger around his collar, he pondered the merits of a high-speed seaside jaunt; then he sighed and regretfully shook his head. "They sounded pretty definite Thoday was squeaky-clean all the time she was with them." He sighed again. "And I don't think we can justify a trip to the other end of the country, no matter how much we fancy a change of scene. We'll just have to rely on the phone and the fax and take people's word for it about her first couple of posts. That's good coppering, my girl. You trust your colleagues to do as thorough a job as you would yourself— and everything's all right."

Both of them appended a two-word rider to this final remark, though neither spoke aloud. The brief silence was broken by Stone.

"Then we could go back to the school, sir. St. Catherine's. If the criminal always returns to the scene of the crime, I don't see why the people investigating it shouldn't, too. Even if," honesty made her add, "I can't think what real use it would do. Our lot finished up there yesterday—"

"Don't I know it!" Trewley groaned with a despairing thump for the heap of folders on his desk.

"But there must be something they've—we've—missed. There must be!"

Trewley looked at her. He dropped the remains of his bun on the plate and brushed crumbs from his hands. "If it'll stop you nagging me, girl, I suppose it wouldn't do any harm. . . ."

She blinked; it was most unlike him to yield without at least a ritual growl of complaint. The cumulative effects of a month's hot weather, no doubt.

"I told you, I fancy a change of scene—but we won't go to the school," he said. So much for that theory. "We'll phone Miss Broome at the council and find out where What's-Her-Name the head cleaner's working right now. We'll go and talk to her again about what happened Thursday evening."

• • •

MRS. AYLIFFE, TO the superintendent's surprise, was at home; his sergeant was less surprised that the little cleaner was not at work as she had been on Friday, when she and Trewley first spoke with her.

"Here I am, then! Got meself a sick note," they were greeted by the tiny figure in the doorway, one hand supporting her against the frame, the other pressed to the middle of her side. "Oh, I can still feel my heart going like a steam-hammer, I really can!" Stone nodded with understanding, while even Trewley, habitual sceptic, had to agree that Mrs. Ayliffe didn't look well.

Indisposition couldn't stop her talking, though. It seemed she was determined to make up—more than make up—for what she hadn't managed to tell them at their original encounter. "You've called about Brenda again," she said, before they had a chance to speak. "You come in, and we'll have a cup of tea. Can't seem to face eating, somehow—oh, poor Brenda, never done no harm to a soul—and of course, with the school still needs cleaning, who's to say it won't be one of us others next?"

She was leading the way indoors as she voiced this bleak thought, and missed both Trewley's indignant splutter and Stone's protesting gasp. "Worried half to death I've been the whole weekend. Never a wink of sleep did I have, couldn't stop *thinking*, as who could blame me, and my heart going bumpety-bump in my head like one o'clock, and when I do drop off it's nightmares—so this morning I went to sign on for the panel and the doctor, she said it come as no surprise to her I was in such a state and I was to have a week off—and that's what I told Miss Broome, not as I took the note all that way round meself, mind you, but I phoned to say I'd got it and she said it'd be all right so long as she gets it by the end of the week."

Circumstances had dictated that it should be Stone, rather than Trewley, who took the lead in Friday's interview. He made no objection when she did so again. "You could ask

one of your neighbours to post it for you, couldn't you?"
Mrs. Ayliffe had explained before that she was a childless
widow. "They'll be rallying round just as soon as they hear
you're a bit under the weather. . . ."

"Weather?" Mrs. Ayliffe crowed with mirth, then winced,
her hand to her side. "Well, dear, this weather don't help,
and that's a fact . . . though they're forecasting thunder
for later on, and that did ought to clear the air, for which I'm
thankful. Might get a decent night's sleep, for once—if it
wasn't for the *dreams*. Just like the telly, only worse
because you can't switch it off." The hand now rose to her
forehead as she massaged her temples. "Poor Brenda—
never to my dying day shall I forget the shock of you pair
turning up at the shop saying as you'd bad news and I'd
better sit down. Kindness itself you was to me that day,
dear."

"I was glad I was able to help," said Stone while Trewley
reiterated a silent prayer of thankfulness that his sidekick
had been medically trained. "And remember, you gave us
almost as much of a shock as we gave you! Which I'd say
makes it quits, Mrs. Ayliffe. You don't need to think about
it any more."

"But I do, dear." The little cleaner shook her head as she
busied herself with teapot and kettle. "And it's not just
because I don't forget a kindness, which ain't my way, but
it's because of poor Brenda. I shan't be able to rest easy until
whoever done this terrible thing to her's been caught and put
away—and I've been thinking, like I said." She reached
absently for a tin the two detectives guessed held biscuits
for the benefit of visitors. If it was true she hadn't eaten
since Friday—and she looked a good deal more frail now
than she'd done four days ago—it would be another act of
kindness for them to encourage her to play the hostess's part
and join her guests in raiding the chocolate digestives.

"You don't take sugar, I dare say." Sparrow-bright eyes
gauged Trewley's likely weight, and Stone's probable concern for her figure. "Me neither, good for shock though they

always say it is, but I'm not giving in to it again, dear, not now I've had some peace and quiet to meself."

"You've been thinking," prompted Stone as Mrs. Ayliffe stirred the pot and held the strainer above the first cup. "Have you . . . thought of anything else that might be of help to me—to us?"

"It was that reporter made me start to wonder." Into the slop-bowl went the strainer, and three cups of leafless tea were set, neatly saucered, on the table.

Stone pushed the tin of biscuits towards Mrs. Ayliffe as the latter took a tentative sip. "Reporter, Mrs. Ayliffe? You mean you've been interviewed by the press? Goodness, how exciting!"

"For the *Argus*," she said with pride. "Come out this week, he said it will, and I get a free copy to keep. Took my picture and all, though if I'd only known I'd have set my hair—but there, we can't always know what's coming to us. And maybe it's best, sometimes, if we don't. . . ."

The biscuits were coffee wafers. Mrs. Ayliffe bit daintily into one, and a sprinkling of flakes showered down on the floral plastic tablecloth. "Like poor Brenda—and that Mrs. Tanner." She tilted her head to one side, favouring her guests with a knowing look. "Didn't strike me, at first. Didn't think nothing of it—well, with the shock and all I wouldn't, would I? But then with the reporter wanting to make a story for the front page—*A Killer Stalks the Street*. After he'd gone it got me thinking, dear. Coincidence is all very well—but two murders in exactly the same place is something else again, ain't it?"

"Yes," Stone agreed softly. Trewley nodded. Both realised they were on the brink of a perhaps vital piece of information. Once broken, the train of Mrs. Ayliffe's thought could be lost forever. . . .

"They got to be connected," said Mrs. Ayliffe. "Logical, that is. And it's logical you'd say it was the school, the connection, on account of 'em both being done in there— but there's coincidence, and coincidence. What's real, and what's . . . fake. Which is what he's banking on, dear. You mark my words, he's only been pretending it's the school. But what's the *likeliest* cause is on account of summat going on with the business as shouldn't be going on, and after Mrs. Tanner found out, so did Brenda, and he knew it—oh, yes," she said as despite their resolve to maintain silence, Trewley and Stone exclaimed in surprise. "Poor Brenda was a good worker. Kept herself busy—and it weren't just the council she cleaned for, with word getting round she could be trusted to do a good job, and needing the money more than most. And if she didn't used to oblige for Mrs. Tanner at that Stitcherie place, well, my name's not Doreen Ayliffe. . . ."

THE THUNDERSTORM THAT broke over Allingham just after six that evening was of monumental proportions. Barometric pressure plummeted; it became almost impossible to breathe; the sky turned grey, then green, then purple, then black. Many in the town supposed Armageddon, Ragnarok, and Götterdämmerung to have joined forces, hellbent on destroying for ever the golden strength of Sol the Supreme in an outburst of elemental fury that chilled the air, soaked the earth, flooded the rivers, and set fire to more than one house—even those fitted with lightning conductors of the celebrated zinc-plated spiral-twist design, guaranteed to stop any streak, any time, no matter where it was bound, and render its errand harmless and its further progress apocryphal. Subsequent investigation by loss adjusters was to show that the installers had failed to use the required silver-tipped fastening points, making do with less efficient copper . . . but this discovery was some weeks in the future. For now, the skies above Allingham boiled and bellowed and blazed in a prodigious climatic cataclysm that had even persons of an exemplary lifestyle wondering what offence they must unwittingly have committed, and how—if spared—they could propitiate their sin.

Detective Sergeant Stone, whose desk was uncomfortably close to the office window, retreated to a far corner of the police canteen, turned her face to the wall, put her fingers in her ears, and refused all succour until the hour of midnight, when a sudden wind arose to drive the storm across the county border. She swallowed three cups of sugared tea in quick succession, voiced her sympathy for the inhabitants of Loamshire, and drove shakily home, unaware that she was being shadowed the entire way by Trewley, whose concern for his young colleague had already caused him to issue stern instructions that she was not to come in next morning until she was absolutely sure she felt up to it.

Throughout that Tuesday, the whole of Allshire yawned, rubbed its eyes, and complained that it had never felt less like work, play, or study in its life. Teachers composed explanatory letters to public examination boards. Retired persons shopped for earplugs and went back to bed. Little of a productive nature was achieved by any paid workers of the county in the hours between eight and five; few were the bosses brave enough to suggest a cut in wages to compensate for this cut in productivity, and even fewer the ones who got away with it. People clocked off on the dot, yawning, and hurried home to an early night. . . .

Claire Summers was still yawning at breakfast on Wednesday. Her parents were disinclined to humour her.

"For pity's sake, stop drooping over your plate like that, Claire. You make anyone feel ill just looking at you—and just look at you!" Alison Summers frowned heavily at her elder daughter. "You haven't even brushed your hair—"

"I have!" Claire scowled and tossed her head. It had taken a lot of effort to achieve the tumbled, windblown, super-model style Some People were stupid enough to mistake for laziness.

"Don't answer your mother back." Richard Summers never raised his eyes from his newspaper. "Finish your breakfast, then go and make yourself tidy. No daughter of mine sits her exams looking like a scarecrow."

"Scarecrow?" Alison tittered at she stabbed the butter with an angry knife. "She looks more like a tramp—and not the worldly-goods-in-a-bundle, stick-over-the-shoulder type, either. If she's not careful, she'll have everyone thinking she's a tart."

Claire turned red. "Strawberry jam or raspberry?" she demanded with another toss of her rich auburn curls.

Muttering an oath, her father dropped the newspaper. "You are not to talk to your mother like that." Alison opened her mouth to say something, but Richard waved her to silence. "You will apologise at once for being so impertinent. Then you will eat the rest of your breakfast without another word."

Further silence: stubborn on Claire's part, resigned on the part of Alison, who shot her husband an eloquent look. "Did you hear me, Claire?"

Claire smothered another yawn. Alison winced.

"Rick, do leave her alone. We haven't time for all that now, if she's supposed to be at school for the exam."

"Good manners are more important than good grades."

"Huh! That's not what you said before."

"If," Richard pressed on, ignoring Claire's interruption, "Claire is serious about this . . . this acting nonsense, she will find theatre managements, like all employers, more willing to offer jobs to those who conduct themselves with restraint and courtesy than to those who mistakenly believe rudeness and hysterical scenes are excused by the so-called artistic temperament."

"It isn't nonsense! I'm good, I know I am, and—"

Once more Claire was ignored as her father's deeper voice drowned out her protests. "Claire will apologise to you, Alison, and she will go to school dressed in an appropriate manner to sit her exams. She will not argue or talk any more nonsense about drama school until she has shown herself capable of acting the part of a reasonable human being offstage as well as on it."

Claire's face—the delicate bone structure inherited from Alison, the sensuous mouth and expressive eyes from the strong-willed Richard—crumpled in a furious scowl; but even fury could not coarsen those features to ugliness. Only a middle-aged father, jealous for his nubile daughter's growing desire to fly the nest, could remain unmoved by her display of passion.

"Did you hear me, Claire?"

"I should think the whole house could hear you." The scowl turned to a sneer. "The whole road, probably."

"Claire! How dare you? Apologise this minute!"

"I won't!"

"Now, you listen to me, young lady!" Richard thumped his fist on the table, slopping half of Alison's tea in its saucer. "Once and for all, I will not have—"

"Be quiet!" The spillage made his wife understandably shrill. "I'm sick to death of you—both of you—arguing and shouting day after day without getting anywhere, neither of you listening to the other, giving me a headache, upsetting Emma . . ."

The same thought occurred at the same time to husband and wife. Emma: their younger daughter, who had for the past three months been a reluctant witness to the mealtime battles between Claire, basking in her undoubted success as Desdemona in the school play, and her parents, who had no wish to see their daughter on the professional stage.

"Emma—she's not down yet." Alison cast an appraising eye at Claire. "I'll just go and call her."

"You're not to spend your life running round after the children. For the amount their education costs, they should at least be able to tell the time." Richard glanced at his watch and frowned: it was later than he'd realised. "There have been enough raised voices in the house this morning. Claire will go up quietly to Emma's room to fetch her," said Claire's father. "Now."

Claire was not only physically attractive and personally ambitious: she was reasonably intelligent, too. She knew how far she could push her luck. She went.

Her parents heard the sullen trudge of her feet up the stairs and the tapping of her fingers on the bedroom door.

They heard her call her sister's name; they heard her tap again, harder.

"Emma. Emma! Are you awake? You're going to be late for school. . . ."

The rattle of the handle, the creak of the hinges. The patter of feet as Claire crossed the room to fling open the curtains . . .

"Emma? Don't be a silly little cow. Come on . . . Emma!"

A rush of feet out of the room, and down the stairs. Into the dining room burst, not the future winner of Oscars and Emmies, but a wide-eyed, startled schoolgirl. "Mum—Dad— she's disappeared. She's gone—she's not there—and I don't think her bed's been slept in!"

Sixteen

A MISSING SCHOOLGIRL, serious though her loss must always be, would in normal circumstances not command the immediate attention of a senior police officer already involved in a double murder investigation.

But this was no normal runaway. The child reported missing was a member of St. Catherine's junior school; and to Detective Superintendent Trewley, scorning coincidence, her disappearance could not be treated independently of other, even more sinister, events of the recent past.

"Only—only twelve," said Alison Summers, choking back a sob. "Twelve last April. We don't have an up-to-date picture—we're waiting for her first official school photo, they take one panorama and two individual shots . . ."

"Twelve years old." Trewley tried not to frown. Twelve years old, missing all night . . . "Has the school taken these snaps yet?"

"Yes, two weeks ago, before the exams started. She was so proud to be in it—she loved—loves—dressing up and disguise—she made me iron her uniform blouse twice that morning before she was satisfied. . . ."

Alison blew her nose discreetly into a handkerchief, and Stone patted her on the shoulder. "Have some more tea," she urged gently. "It will help you think. We'll get on to the school photographers, of course, but to save time, you are sure you haven't even a little snap we could use?"

Alison blinked at the sergeant through her tears. "She . . .

not in the last year or so. She's always been a funny self-conscious little thing, not like her sister, and once all the fuss about the play started last autumn she was even more . . ." Her mouth twisted sideways in misery. Or guilt?

"We gave her a camera last birthday, but she was—is— much more interested in taking photos than in having anyone use it to take photos of her. She photographs the strangest things—not scenery, not sunsets, or animals— none of the things you'd expect from a child her age . . . but people—complete strangers—and cars, and bicycles— and shoes, dozens of shoes . . ."

Emma Summers no doubt believed, as did all runaways of whatever age, that her reasons for leaving home were valid. By her standards, they might well be; but even Stone, with her medical background, would hate to guess the child's likely plans using her apparent psychological state as a basis for reasoning.

"Does she have any friends?"

Alison hesitated. "It was . . . difficult for her, having an elder sister at the same school. We'd imagined it would help her—she's never been much of a mixer, always reading and daydreaming by herself. . . . We hoped it would make her feel more comfortable, more confident at St. Catherine's—it's so much larger than her primary school . . . but Claire is such a very pretty girl—so popular with everyone. And so lively . . ."

It was a melancholy picture Alison Summers was paint-ing. Stone's heart went out to young Emma, in every way far less attractive—that was clear—than her elder sister, feeling alone, unloved, unwanted as only a shy child can feel. . . . "One special crony, perhaps? Somebody she'd be on the phone to as soon as she came home, even if they'd just spent all day in the same classes?"

"I'm afraid not, Sergeant. Poor Emma—but she seemed happy enough. . . ." Emma's mother choked, then blushed as she caught Stone exchange a quick glance with Trewley.

"No, she wasn't." Alison sounded almost relieved to be able to say it out loud. "Happy, I mean. Not really . . . I can see that now—but while she was putting up such a—a brave front I suppose we were just grateful . . . we've been so busy worrying about Claire, and her nonsensical idea of giving up school to go on the stage, to . . . to . . ."

"To pay much attention to the one who wasn't throwing a tantrum all the time?" It was Trewley who spoke. Poor kid. With three of his own he understood only too well how it could be the devil's own job to give each one a fair share of his time and effort: but it had to be done. You couldn't just forget about the quiet one because she wasn't causing you any grief right then. Odds on she was bottling it all up inside, and would let it out with an almighty roar one day before too long. . . .

Like Emma Summers. "No friends," he said heavily. "Her sister, now. Would you say they were close? A big age difference, is there?"

"Claire is sixteen and very mature for her age. Emma is . . . very young for twelve. They didn't—don't—have a great deal in common, I'm afraid. I doubt if she—if either of them—would confide in the other."

"Nose a bit out of joint? Young Emma, I mean." Trewley spoke with the voice of experience. "Popular sister, some-one to live up to, new school—quarrels at home about big sister's career—you and your husband worried sick natu-rally, but Emma thinks you're more bothered about your favourite daughter—not that I'm suggesting for a minute she is—than about her . . ."

Alison had turned pale. Her eyes widened in sockets already dark with worry, and she spoke through quivering lips. "Yes, Superintendent. I'm ashamed to say that's exactly how it must have appeared to Emma—and we never even noticed! How awful . . . it's unforgivable . . ."

She buried her face in her hands. Once more, Stone patted her gently on the shoulder. As Alison at last stopped shuddering. "Did she ever," enquired Stone, "ask you if she was adopted?"

Alison shot up. "How did you know that?" Her face was now white with terror, her voice shrill. "Don't say she's been to the police with such a—a ridiculous story!" She gulped. "I simply couldn't bear. . . ."

"It's a common enough fantasy," Stone said in soothing tones, "among children who feel a little . . . neglected—whether or not there's any good reason for them to feel that way," she added quickly. "It fits in beautifully with the daydreaming, the solitary life, the apart-ness she feels—it explains everything. Her parents don't understand her *because they aren't her real parents*! So she needn't feel guilty about being angry with them—it's the best excuse in the world, and makes her a good deal happier than she might otherwise be."

"Except," Trewley reminded them as Alison began to look almost hopeful, "that she can't have been all that happy the last day or so, at least, to have taken off the way she's done. Did anything in particular happen last night? Scolding from her parents? Squabble with her sister? Couldn't do her homework and afraid to go to school today?"

Alison shifted on her chair. "She was having a little difficulty with her sewing—such close work, when her eyes were so tired—but I was able to help her, and she finished in time. She won't have been worried about that, I'm sure."

"Umph." Trewley didn't push the needlework connection; he and Stone could consider it later, in private. "Has she said anything about being bullied?"

"St. Catherine's is a very good school. Nothing of that sort would be allowed, I'm sure." Alison spoke sharply, her misery for the moment forgotten.

"People don't always know what's going on under their noses—or just beyond them," said Trewley grimly. "It might not be other kids at the same school who are the bullies, Mrs. Summers. The St. Catherine's girls are a sitting target for some of the yob element, with that posh uniform. There have been one or two cases of kids from the secondary modern picking on youngsters who're too scared, or too well brought up, to stand up to the little perishers and give 'em as much lip as they get. . . ."

"Nothing like that, Superintendent, I'm sure. That is," she said, remembering how sure she'd been of other things, "as far as I know. She was tired last night—yawning, saying she'd go to bed as soon as she'd finished her prep—but that's hardly a surprise, after the sleepless night everyone had on Monday. Richard—my husband—and I were tired, too—and so was Claire, though with her exams that's not surprising, either. Even if she hadn't said she was tired—and she went up only half an hour or so after Emma—we have always insisted that she has an early night before each paper, and doesn't stay up late trying to revise. Anything she crams in at the last minute will only confuse her. . . ."

"She's sitting an exam today?" There had to be some good reason for the poor woman to have been left alone—no husband (work, she'd explained: an important meeting), no daughter—at such a time.

"History, this afternoon. But I insisted she go in this morning as usual, so that she wouldn't . . . lose her concentration when . . . the police got here. She can't tell you anything, Superintendent, I'm sure. . . ." She remembered other surenesses, and hesitated before adding, "I—we, that is, Richard and I—meant it for the best. For her future—qualifications are so important . . ."

"But she doesn't think so." Trewley rubbed his chin. "You say you've been arguing about this on and off since the autumn?" A very long time for a sensitive child, forced to hear even if she tries not to listen.

"It was *Othello* that caused all the trouble," Alison said bitterly. "The new theatre—that wretched bequest. The school would never have tried anything so ambitious, I'm sure, if it hadn't been for that. . . ."

St. Catherine's had always prided itself on the rounded education it gave its pupils, many of whom went on to distinguish themselves in later life. One of the most distin-

guished of many distinguished Katies was the actress Dame
Carolyn Armistead, who chose to celebrate her elevation to
the peerage by making a more than generous monetary
donation to her old school, on condition that the money be
used for the erection of a custom-built theatre. Dame
Carolyn wrote to her old headmistress, Miss Waide, that
while she had fond memories of St. Catherine's as a school,
she remembered far less fondly the inconveniences of the
school hall in its Converted Theatre mode.

Miss Waide was thrilled by the success of her protégée,
and on her behalf embraced with fervour the New Theatre
project. Despite opposition from many quarters—including
the conservationists and public footpath users whose activi-
ties had caused the police some concern—the Carolyn
Armistead Theatre had given its first production at the end
of the spring term. Making every use of excellent facilities,
Othello had played with lavish costumes, elaborate scenery,
and masterly lighting to full houses night after night.

"Claire was Desdemona." Even at such a moment, Alison
couldn't help a note of pride creeping into her voice. "She's
lovely to look at, of course, but I have to admit she really
made a good job of the part, compared to the other girl.
Perhaps she *could* go on to do it professionally, I don't
know—but sixteen is far too young to leave school,
especially when it could just have been a fluke. Only . . ."

"Only she didn't see it like that." Trewley recalled his
neighbour's daughter, and the *Allingham Argus* review. "An
acute case of swelled head for Miss Claire, then, caught in
the spring and still going strong. And young Emma left on
the sidelines to sulk?"

"Oh, she's not a sulky child, Superintendent. Moody, you
could say, though that's nothing remarkable in teenage
girls . . ." Trewley nodded. Alison never noticed: she was
thinking aloud. "Thoughtful. Quiet . . ."

The superintendent did not voice the observation that it was
often the quiet ones who merited most watching, though he

guessed that Stone was considering the same point. He sighed, cleared his throat, and lumbered to his feet.

"We'll take a look at her bedroom now, if we may. See if she's left any sort of clue about where she might have gone." *And who she might have gone with . . .* but this was another thought he did not voice aloud.

The years at medical college, followed by her experiences as a serving police officer, had left Stone feeling wise beyond her years. She hadn't realised, however, just how far she was out of touch with the younger generation until she stood on the threshold of Emma's bleak little bedroom.

"No posters?" She stared. "No cuddly toys?"

"She . . . got rid of them," said Alison, "when she turned twelve. She told me she was too old for them, and to give them to . . . to a charity shop, of all places. But I . . . I couldn't bring myself to do it."

Alison shivered, though it was hard to tell whether her distress was caused by the very idea of entering a charity shop or by some more serious emotion. There was an uncomfortable silence. "It seemed so . . . final," she said at last. "Brutal. Ending her childhood so . . . so soon . . ."

An idea began to chime faintly in the very farthest recesses of the sergeant's brain, drowning out the resonance of that most uncomfortable thought. "Did she ever check up on you—ask what you'd done with them?"

Alison smiled a watery smile. "She said she knew I hadn't done what she asked, because she'd looked in Oxfam and the other places and hadn't seen a single toy." The smile faded. "I—I'm afraid I didn't tell her the truth, Sergeant. I said I'd been . . . worried it would upset her to see them on sale, and I'd slipped across to Sayersleigh one market day and given them to cancer research. . . ."

"I take it none of her fellow Katies come from Sayersleigh," said Stone. "She wouldn't be able to check, right?"

Alison nodded. "I knew at least that much about her classmates—but I knew—know—nothing about Emma,

Sergeant. Nothing! If I had, how could I have let her run away like this?"

"Let's just see what she's taken with her," said Stone as Emma's mother began shivering again. "No favourite toys, that's obvious." She contemplated the neatly ranked bookshelves: there were no gaps. She moved across to study some of the titles, drew in a sharp breath, and earned a quick look from Trewley. Before he could speak, she went on:

"Clothes, Mrs. Summers. What's she likely to have been wearing? And where did she keep her camera?"

Alison's hands clasped and unclasped repeatedly as she sank, still shivering, on the edge of her daughter's bed. "Her camera's in her desk, but . . . her clothes—I . . . I haven't been able to bring myself to look. Claire—my husband— they both say that couldn't find anything gone beyond her light jacket, and the things she changed into after school yesterday, but . . ."

The chime was louder now. Stone said, "Do you mean light as in colour—or light as in weight?" And she had a strong suspicion which guess would be correct.

"We didn't approve of a child her age wearing black, but Claire has one—and when Emma said she wanted it— insisted everyone else wore them, which they do—so ugly . . ."

Stone sighed. "Wanted, Mrs. Summers, or needed?" Trewley looked at her again. Alison, frowning, hesitated.

"Now you mention it . . . she sounded so strange, but . . . she said she *needed* a black jacket, Sergeant. She was just about willing to accept navy blue, but . . ."

"Ah," said Trewley in a neutral tone as his sergeant opened the wardrobe door without comment. "These casual clothes—jeans, of course. And?"

"T-shirt, with a blouse over it later. It's been so much cooler in the evening since the storm."

"Shoes?" Stone looked at the wardrobe floor. "No, that age group prefers trainers. Yes?"

"Yes, Sergeant."

"Money," said Trewley, trying not to sound alarmist. "Piggy bank, building society, post office savings?"

Alison blinked. "She'd just opened a savings account with what was left over from her birthday. She tried to put in something every week, but it wasn't much—most of her pocket money went on her books and her photography. Richard keeps the savings book in his desk—she asks him when she wants to use it—and he thought of that," she added as the inevitable question hovered on Trewley's lips. "Before he left for work, he found time to check in his desk. The drawer was still locked, and her savings book was inside."

With the inference that the girl had made no unusual withdrawals recently. Brooding, Trewley rubbed his chin. What about unusual deposits? Motherly love was all very well, but in a case like this, where he'd risk a bet the line Stone had tacitly suggested was the right one, they couldn't take anything on trust.

"We'll look at the book later, if you don't mind. Just to satisfy ourselves," he said as Alison's mouth opened to protest that Richard wouldn't like it, and in any case the key was with him at work. "But for now, to sum up, it seems your daughter left the house last night—or whenever it was—wearing the same clothes she wore yesterday, taking nothing with her that we can immediately spot, including money. The last time you saw her she was in a normal frame of mind, and there are no signs of a struggle," he said, glancing around the almost obsessively tidy room. "We have to conclude, Mrs. Summers, that she left of her own accord—and that wherever she went, she didn't go far."

"And she meant to come back," supplied Alison in a whisper. "Before we knew she'd gone. And . . . and then something—must have happened—to prevent her . . ."

"It looks like that," said Trewley, "but appearances can be deceptive, you know. These girls, they play tricks on people. They're young: they don't realise how hurtful and worrying it can be to an adult. She could be hiding out in a den in the woods, something of that sort. Worn out, over-slept, ricked her ankle hurrying and couldn't get home—oh, she could come hopping in on crutches any minute, after some good Samaritan's whipped her off to casualty for a checkup—and probably given her a piece of his mind, as well."

Alison tried to smile. "Like the lorry driver." There had been a recent incident between a long-distance driver and a runaway hitchhiker that had given several people pause for thought. The hitcher, a fifteen-year-old girl, had spent the entire journey complaining that her parents mistreated her, didn't understand her, and had outgrown any possible use to her. She was old enough to look after herself, whatever they said, and once she reached London she'd prove it to them, the antiquated fools.

Her chauffeur eyed his nubile passenger in silence for a while, then drove the lorry off the road into a secluded lay-by, screened by trees from any sight of passing traffic. He had ignored the girl's gasps of horror, seized her in a powerful grasp, turned her over his knee, and given her a spanking she would never forget. She was no more capable of looking after herself (he told her) than a babe in arms; he had two daughters himself, and knew what he was talking about. And if she didn't that instant tell him her name and address, he would deliver her to the nearest police station and give her in charge as a vagrant.

The girl's parents had been astounded by the change in their rebellious child. Sobbing with repentance, she told them her story. Her father gripped the driver firmly by the hand, and between his own sobs swore eternal gratitude. Her mother hailed the driver as a hero and sent the runaway off to the shops for witch hazel for her bruises. The episode ended happily.

But as for Emma Summers . . .

And Stone, poring once more over the selection of books on Emma's shelves, uttered an exclamation as her eye was caught by a movement outside the window, in the street. The movement of a car slowing down as it reached the Summers house . . . pulling in to the kerb . . . parking . . .

The movement of a car door opening, and someone climbing out. Someone walking to the Summers gate and up the front path to the door.

Someone in police uniform . . .

───────── Seventeen ─────────

THE MOOD AMONG staff and senior pupils of St. Catherine's was still subdued, though all signs of the necessary police presence had been removed two days earlier. For the elder members of the little community it was certainly no case of out of sight, out of mind: the unsolved killings were never far from people's thoughts, and were, moreover, not their only worries. There were exams to sit or to supervise; there were last-minute panics to soothe or to overcome.

For junior Katies, like their elders unable to forget the two murders that had been committed in their school, the atmosphere was more one of suppressed excitement than of thoughtful solemnity. What had happened, despite having been on television and in the papers, did not—somehow could not—concern them greatly. They were living in the middle of a real-life detective story, but it was nothing to do with them.

Several remembered Lois Tanner from having accompanied their mothers shopping in Stitcherie, one or two could put a face to the name of Brenda French; but as the cleaners tended to clean after school hours, it was no surprise that even Brenda's fate should not affect any child in any serious way. For one another's benefit, the juniors gaily embellished stories about pale midnight flickerings of spectral flame above the school buildings; they whispered of ghostly forms heard wailing aloud for vengeance, and enjoyed themselves immensely as they shivered with delicious fright, and gave the needlework room—unlocked as of Monday morning on the orders of Miss Thoday—a deliberately wide berth.

Yet it was not all hauntings and horrors. The animal spirits of the young, no matter what the circumstances, are seldom for long suppressed, and the youngest Katies were no exception to this rule. They were as constitutionally incapable of remaining quiet as a litter of puppies.

Nevertheless, they were quieter than they would have wished. While Monday's storm had cleared the air, by this Wednesday morning the welcome coolness that had followed was a faded memory. Well before the eleven o'clock break, it was too hot to run around. When one sturdy maiden produced a tennis ball and proposed a game of Sunday, Monday, there arose the first peal of spontaneous laughter anyone had heard on the St. Catherine's premises for nearly a week.

"Then we'll sit somewhere in the shade and play Clap-and-Bounce." Young Karen, assuming her habitual role of leader—the ball was, in any case, hers—surveyed the area with a quick and knowledgeable eye. It was time to reassert her authority. "The sun won't be past *that* bit until after we've gone back indoors." She pointed a finger, daring anyone to speak against her choice.

The shadow cast by the New Building across the asphalt playground turned its demure rose tint to a dusky crimson beneath the windows of the needlework room, a silent memorial to blood recently shed nearby. Darker shadows among the whispering leaves of the shrubbery promised secret revelations for those who would dare to listen. . . .

"Come on, then!" Karen trotted off without once turning back to see if her friends were with her. If she saw that they weren't, she would lose her nerve—and a leader who loses her nerve doesn't stay leader for long. Karen walked on, bouncing the ball from hand to ground to hand in an intrepid triangle, whistling as she walked.

Her cronies were not to be outdone by their captain, and

they knew there was safety in numbers. They also knew that
the charge of cowardice, once hurled, would be hard to
deny. Juveniles have as healthy a respect for the power of
popular opinion as any adult politician . . . and the rest of
Karen's gang scampered after her, drawing close, but not
overtaking—just in case.

With squeals and giggles the little group seated themselves in the required circle. "I'll start," said Karen, as if
there had been any doubt. "None." She threw the ball to her
neighbour, who caught it deftly.

"None." Andrea threw to Susan.

"None . . . None . . . None . . ." Susan to Rachel,
Rachel to Louise, Louise to Tillie, until the circle was
complete, and Karen caught the ball with a triumphant,
"One!"

Andrea just had time to clap before the ball was in her
hands. "One!" Andrea to Susan. "One!" Susan to Rachel,
Rachel to Louise, Louise to Tillie . . .

"Two!" Caller Karen was allowed to choose when the
more difficult Bounce should be added to the game. By
tossing the ball high, it was sometimes possible to clap as
many as six times before the plain Throw was abandoned.
The children had no idea that Clap-and-Bounce improved
their hand, eye, and brain coordination: they only knew that
it was fun to play, especially when a mistimed throw or a
miscaught catch sent the next player tumbling backwards to
the mocking laughter of her friends. This time round,
however, they only reached four before they had to stop.

"Bounce none!" Karen to Andrea, Andrea to Susan . . .

"Bounce one!" . . . Bounce two!" It was going well.
Was this to be an all-time record, against which future
generations of infant Katies would set themselves in vain?

"Bounce three! Oh, butterfingers!"

"Andrea butter, Andrea butter, born and bred and bread in
the gutter!" came the ritual chant as Andrea groaned and
crawled into the bushes. "You didn't have to throw so hard,"

she complained, as lower less leafy twigs scratched her bare arms and legs. "Ow! My hair!"

"Hurry up, stupid. The bell will go in a minute. . . ."

"It's all dark in here, and there are spiders. I don't like it." Andrea reversed smartly and emerged, blinking, into the relative brightness of the sunlit shade. "I couldn't see it, anyway—and who are you calling stupid? You threw it, so you can fetch it if you're so clever."

Karen knew when gracious surrender was moral strength. "I'll find it in no time," she said with a confidence that impressed as she'd known it would. "I watched where it was going, for a start."

Smoothing the pleats of her blue gingham frock over her knees, she plunged into the shrubbery, pushing her way along a path parallel to that taken by Andrea, but—to her surprise—finding it easier to negotiate the tangled twiggy gloom than her friend had done. There were no spiders' webs to smear her face: it was almost as if someone else had been there first. . . .

They had.

And they were still there. Suddenly ahead of her, curled in an almost hide-and-seek pose, a small figure revealed itself to Karen's searching gaze. It did not boast the familiar pale gleam of the Katies' junior uniform with its tiny checks in white and blue; it wore—was wrapped in—the dark covering of a casual jacket, while a trainer-shod foot was visible at the end of one trailing leg clad in universal denim.

Karen caught her breath. She felt cold. This person . . . was very still, for hide-and-seek. Wasn't moving even enough to stir nearby leaves with her breath. . . .

"Trespassers!" she cried in shrill bravado. "Spies!" One of the secondary modern kids, that's who it was, playing truant, come to make fools of the Katie crowd. . . .

The intruder made no move to submit to superior forces. Did not move . . . Did not breathe. *Was only acting* . . .

From outside came the welcome voices of her friends.

"What's wrong, Karen? Who's trespassing? Have you caught a spy? Who is it?"

Only acting. *Wasn't she?* Karen licked her lips. She could not speak. Her throat was dry; her head was hot and clammy. Her hands were cold. She shivered. She tried to move forward to confirm official capture of the enemy . . . and tried . . .

In the far distance, above the ringing in her ears, she heard the ringing of a bell. Its familiar clamour sounded strangely muffled. Unfocused. Unreal . . .

"Karen—the bell! Stop playing now, and we can come back later. Do hurry up!"

Andrea's voice rose above the rest and galvanised her friend to action. Karen braced herself to crawl another two steps. Her hand, shaking, reached out to touch the jacket of the stranger.

"Got you." It should have been a cry of victory: it was more like a squeak. She tried again. "Got you!"

"Karen, come on, or there'll be such a row. If you want to play spies, we can do it after dinner. . . ."

Karen tugged at the jacket. She tugged harder. Nothing moved except her hand, her arm. . . .

And then the flap and rustle of the jacket unwrapping from under the wearer . . .

And then the horrid, hollow thump as she rolled over and turned her face to the leafy fastness overhead.

A face with staring eyes and open mouth. A face smudged with earth in a way no living face could bear . . .

Karen began to scream.

THE OCCASION WAS far too grim for anyone to try lightening it with some feeble witticism about taking up residence, or the need for a parking permit. For the third time in seven days the complete forensic team was assembled in St. Catherine's School—and not, this third unlucky time, for the death of an adult.

"Twelve years old." Trewley tore his mind away from his

own happy family to ponder the tragedy of Emma Summers. "Twelve, and never going to see thirteen—it makes me sick. If I could get my hands on him—"

"Or her." Stone sighed. "It didn't look as if the poor little thing was sexually assaulted, so I suppose it could be either. . . ."

"Him or her, I only wish—but there." Trewley sighed and shuffled his feet as if trying to obliterate his wayward thoughts. Then he cursed at the realisation of what else he might be obliterating, and moved away from the shrubbery to a spot still in view of the professional hubbub, but out of earshot of the professionals.

"You might not be talking nonsense, at that," he said after a long pause, during which he rubbed his chin and stared back into the recent past. "Miss Thoday, now . . ."

The headmistress had apparently taken charge almost immediately the screams of young Karen alerted those in classrooms close by that something serious had occurred. While the child and her terrified friends were whisked, on Avis's orders, to the school's sick bay, the curious girls peering from windows to learn what was happening were sent back to their studies by one curt command from Miss Thoday. Discipline at St. Catherine's, even during Miss Waide's time, was strong; and the new head's reputation was not one of a woman inclined to lenience. Teachers in those classes that had been interrupted by the outcry shook in their mental shoes for fear of what would be said to them later about Poor Discipline; and their chastened pupils, once more obediently seated at their desks, speculated in a thrilled silence as to what on earth might be going on in the playground outside the needlework room.

The police, contrary to general opinion, seldom arrive at the scene of a crime with sirens blaring and blue lights flashing. The same restraint does not, however, apply to the men of the ambulance service, whose view—rightly—is that, while there is any chance of life, there is hope, and with that hope a consequent need for haste. The nine-nine-nine

call to St. Catherine's had been placed not by Avis, who
would have been crisp, efficient, and nonalarmist, but by
Kathleen Shorey, who was . . . none of those things.

It had irked the headmistress to be forced to delegate, but
even the efficient Miss Thoday must acknowledge that she
could not be in two places at once. Anyone (within reason)
could use a telephone, and it would soon become apparent
if that telephone had not been used. On the other hand,
while attention was elsewhere . . . .

A trustworthy guard must be posted at the scene of
the . . . incident. And whom could Avis Thoday trust
better than herself? She would be that guard, although for
her own protection she would keep two members of staff
with her. Whether she hoped thus to protect her person
(from the risk that the murderer might return) or her
reputation (alone with the evidence) she would not, even in
her innermost thoughts, admit. She dismissed the other
teachers, warning them that they were on no account to
permit exaggerated word of the Incident to spread among
their pupils.

"We will wait for the police," insisted Miss Thoday. "It
will be their decision how much, or how little, of what has
happened is made known. . . ."

But the ambulance arrived before the police, its siren
blaring, its blue lights flashing as it raced to what might still
be the rescue.

And within minutes the whole of St. Catherine's, whether
closeted in an examination room or at liberty to giggle and
whisper and exclaim behind upturned textbooks, knew—or
could hazard a fair guess at—more or less everything that
was going on in the New Building playground, outside the
needlework room.

HER CLASSMATES HAD barely noticed the absence of Emma
Summers. With no close friends and few acquaintances, she
merged into the background with a melancholy success, and
had been automatically marked Absent on the morning

register. Even her form mistress saw no cause for concern: this near the end of term it was not unknown for younger Katies, with few exams to worry them, to suffer mild attacks of hay fever which freed them from lessons for a day or two. Emma might be a reserved, rather lonely child, but clearly she had absorbed more of the St. Catherine's ethic than had been realised.

Her sister had maintained an uncharacteristic silence on Emma's disappearance. The sight of the empty bedroom had startled Claire Summers, but being sent to school as usual made her assume at first that there was little seriously wrong. If her parents were worried, wouldn't they have shown it? For all her claims to maturity, she was too young to appreciate how the British dislike of making a fuss, with the traditional desire to carry on regardless, can be taken, on occasion, to extremes. Richard, from whom his elder daughter had inherited her thespian talents, left for his meeting only five minutes after the appointed hour; Alison blinked back frightened tears with resolution, and only telephoned the police once Claire had been waved on her way to school.

It was during the half-mile walk to St. Catherine's that Claire began for the first time to think. Younger sisters, she had always felt, were a pain. They got in the way and unfairly held you back when you were trying to spread your wings and your parents meanly used them as an excuse to keep you a little girl forever. You were supposed to Set a Good Example by being older, but you weren't allowed to *be* older, to make your own decisions like a proper, responsible adult with the right to choose what to do with her life.

Claire paused to stroke a ginger cat as sleek and self-possessed as she believed herself to be. The cat, lazing in the sun, flattened its ears and purred luxuriantly. Claire sighed with envy and walked on.

She'd done her best to reason with the Wrinklies, but the older generation always thought they knew it all—and did they listen? Did they, hell! What could they know about life the way it was lived *now*, not thirty years ago when they were young—if they'd ever been young, which she doubted. If they had, they would have *understood* without all the . . . fuss. There wouldn't have been so many arguments day after boring day—and Dad saying he'd lock her in her room until she saw sense was taking things *too far*. But that was just like parents. Unreasonable. She shouldn't have had to wear herself out slogging for stupid exams she knew she'd never need. She wouldn't have had to . . .

Oh. All at once, self-centered Claire wondered whether Emma's disappearance might—possibly—have anything to do with her.

From wondering she fell quietly to worrying: so quietly, indeed, that on arrival at school, absorbed in her thoughts, she passed up her chance for the Big Scene any natural actress would have realised.

And when the screaming started, to be followed inevitably by fuss and commotion and wildest rumour, she worried all the more.

And when someone in authority came looking for her, to tell her there was trouble at home and her parents would have bad news to break . . .

Claire Summers, like her sister, had disappeared.

Eighteen

"I ALWAYS HATE this bit." The superintendent walked slowly up the path, his hands deep in his pockets not from forensic necessity, but from social embarrassment. "However you break the news, it's still . . . bloody."

"People say you get used to anything, in time." Stone kicked out at an imaginary pebble on the immaculate crazy-paving. "I can't say I've noticed it."

"Umph." Trewley paused at the door for one moment and sighed. "Well . . . quick and clean's the best way, in the end," he said and reached out to press the bell.

Before his finger had made the connection, the door was wrenched open by Alison Summers, her face pale within the delicate aureole of her light auburn hair. "You've found her? Is she all right—is she hurt? Where is she?"

"May we come in, Mrs. Summers?"

Alison's eyes widened, staring in silent, awful anticipation of what was to come. Her former pallor was a healthy bloom compared to the sickly yellow-green tinge that now touched even her lips. The hand that still held the open door tightened its grip until the knuckles were white. She swayed, closed her eyes, and took several deep, shuddering breaths before opening them again.

"It's . . . bad news, isn't it?"

"If you'd just let us in, Mrs. Summers. Please."

Alison did not move. She licked her lips. Her voice came in a croaking whisper. "She's . . . dead?"

Quick and clean. "I'm sorry, Mrs. Summers. Yes."

Stone leaped forward, seized Alison around the waist, and pushed her back into the hall towards the stairs. She supported the swaying woman until her knees had finished buckling, then, seated on the lowest step to support her, thrust her patient's head between her knees. "Water," she directed as Trewley closed the door and mopped his brow. "The kitchen's through there, I should think."

It was: her detective skills had not misled her; but those of Trewley were a little less acute when faced with the cupboards and miscellaneous containers of another. By the time the superintendent at last reappeared with a glass in his hand, Alison was emerging from her faint and trying, through teeth that chattered horribly, to beg the sergeant's pardon for having made such an exhibition of herself.

Stiff upper lip was all very well, but there were times when it could be a positive curse. Stone put her arm around her patient's shoulders and gave her a hug.

"Don't apologise, Mrs. Summers. There's no need—and no need to bottle it all up, either. You've had a shock, and it will be much better for you in the long run if you give in to the worst of it now."

She was not so foolish as to try persuading the woman that one good bout of weeping would cure the hurt of that shock. It would ease it, she knew, as far as anything could—but, while the immediate pain and distress might fade, they would never in her life again entirely forsake the sorrowing mother. To lose any loved one must always be a cause of grief; to lose one by violence is a tragedy. And for violence to strike down a child is, for the parents, tragedy beyond description . . .

"How . . ." Alison sipped at the water Stone held to her lips. Against her teeth, the glass rattled. "How did . . ." She took another sip, then raised a tremulous hand to push the glass away. "How did it happen?"

The sergeant looked at the superintendent, looming

unhappily nearby. He sighed. *Quick and clean.* "She was stabbed, Mrs. Summers."

A little gasping cry.

Stone said quickly: "Please, Mrs. Summers—"

"Stabbed?" Alison's tone was hollow. "Stabbed . . ." In her throat, a muscle twitched and jumped. "Was it . . . would it have been . . . quick?" Her eyes were fixed on Trewley: she paid no heed to Stone. "Was she . . . did she have time to be . . . frightened?"

What could he say? "We don't have all the details yet, Mrs. Summers, but we . . . do believe it was quick. And," he said before she could ask anything more awkward, "there was no sign of sexual assault."

Alison buried her face in her hands.

They let her weep for a while, Trewley in an agony of impatient indecision until Stone, with a nod, gave him permission to go on.

"Mrs. Summers, I think your husband ought to be with you. If you can tell us where he works, I can arrange—"

"Oh, no!" It was the first sign of life she had shown. "No, Richard will be so . . ." She swallowed. "His meeting, you see—that's why he had to go to work today in the first place. They're . . . important clients, from abroad. He'll be taking them to lunch afterwards, and . . ."

Stone gritted her teeth. What these disjointed remarks said about the home life of the Summers children, the doormat nature of their mother, and the head of the household's Simon Legree complex would have had card-carrying feminists spitting feathers with rage.

"Mrs. Summers, if it's at all possible, he really ought to be here." Trewley raised a mournful eyebrow at his sergeant, who frowned, contemplated the back of Alison's head, then nodded. "You see," he said bravely, "I'm sorry, but . . . it isn't just Emma we've come about."

Stone felt Alison stiffen within her kindly grasp. She continued to hold her as the superintendent went on: "It's Claire, as well. No," he said as Alison uttered a cry, "not dead." He did not add the monstrous rider inevitably uppermost in everyone's thoughts. "But missing, I'm afraid. It seems the news about Emma got round the school much faster than anyone had expected—they'd tried to keep it dark, but with the police swarming all over the place, and the ambu—"

"The school?" Alison latched on to the one piece of information that seemed familiar to her in her shocked state. "You mean Emma was . . . you mean—it—happened up at St. Catherine's?"

"She was found there, yes." No more than half a mile from home. Half a mile from safety.

Or . . . was home so safe? Statistically, you were more likely to be despatched to another spiritual plane by your nearest, if not dearest. Husbands and wives, parents and children . . . How many wayward teenagers had been shaken into what their irate fathers called sense and, in that shaking, had died? There was a case only the year before of a man who, despairing his daughter's late hours and wild friends, had lain in wait for her on her return after a riotous night out; who had confronted her in a fury and seen her crumple, suddenly unconscious, terrified by his wrath. The girl had felt sick with fright—had *been* sick—had choked to death in her father's loving grasp . . . and he had been left lamenting, bewildered, and panic-stricken.

He'd been found out in the end, of course; and what had made his sentence even more severe had been the fact that he hadn't called at once for help, but had done his best to conceal his crime by hiding the body in the middle of Hannasyde Heath, and telling everyone the girl had left home in a fit of temper after a blazing row.

Was it now to be a case of history repeating itself?

"Your husband," said Trewley again as Alison clearly struggled to come to terms with this whole new, transformed, unrecognisable world. "We do want to talk to him, Mrs. Summers—and to you, naturally. But it would be better if you weren't alone."

"Claire," said Alison, staring straight ahead. "She and

Richard—I know it must have upset poor little Emma . . . so many quarrels . . . And now Claire's run away, too?"

It was clear they weren't going to get much out of her that was useful until the initial shock had worn off. "We'd like to hazard a guess to where she might have gone, Mrs. Summers." Three daughters had left Trewley not unacquainted with the sometimes tortuous workings of the teenage mind. "Her friends, I take it, will all be at school. Now, does she have any older folk she could trust? Folk who're at work all the time, perhaps got to know 'em through a Saturday job, while the younger ones—"

"Richard disapproves of children working while they are still at school." Alison blinked. "Not even a holiday job. He says children are children and ought to concentrate on their studies. There's time enough for them to learn about income tax and managing your finances later, when . . ."

Tears welled up in her eyes and spilled over to her cheeks. With the back of her hand, she brushed them away, but they welled up still faster. She ignored them. "There wasn't nearly enough time for Emma, was there, Mr. Trewley? And now . . . if—if Claire . . ."

"We'd like to search her room—both rooms," he said quickly as Alison let a sob escape her, and he feared the worst. "For, uh, clues, as I said. Girls that age, they'll keep a diary. Hidden, of course, and most of it romantic daydreaming nonsense—but enough real-life stuff in it to give us an idea of the . . . the more private bits of their lives." He rubbed his chin and sighed. "Got to find the diaries first, of course, so if you've no objection—it'll help us no end. . . ."

They left Alison downstairs, warming cold hands around the cup of strong, sweet tea Stone had made after coaxing her hostess into the kitchen to supervise her makeshift efforts among the multitude of cupboards.

"There's nothing more we can do for Emma bar catch her killer, God willing," Trewley said, "but while there's life, there's hope—and what I'm hoping is we find young Claire before the same thing happens to her." He paused. "If it hasn't already, that is." He braced himself. "We'll check her room first, Stone. Emma can wait—every second counts at a time like this."

He ushered her through the open door of what a weeping Alison had described as unmistakably Claire's room: and Claire's mother had not been wrong. There was no mistaking the influence of stage and screen on the starstruck teenager. Posters of stills from classic black-and-white films covered one wall; a faded print of the Millais *Ophelia*, blown up to giant size, was framed above the bed, while Mrs. Siddons as Lady Macbeth emoted at the drowning unfortunate from the opposite wall. A mobile hung above the window, and close inspection showed that the shapes spinning gently in the draught were heroines from Shakespeare: Juliet on her balcony, Rosalind and Viola swaggering in masculine attire, Portia in her lawyer's robes, Desdemona with the betraying handkerchief in her bewildered grasp.

"Split personality, sir?" Stone was examining the books ranged along the windowsill and piled beside the bed. Here were no sober treatises on the actor's art, no lengthy tomes of reminiscence, but garish paperbacks of Hollywood biographies, filled with scandal and sexual boasting. "Or a later development? These look more . . . recent than the serious stuff." She nodded towards Ophelia, whose tragedy had been softened by a thin layer of dust. "When Daddy said No, she gave up the idea of trying for the National Theatre and decided to . . . to go quick and commercial instead."

"Umph." The superintendent considered this possibility as he gazed at the well-thumbed pages and cracked spines of Claire's favourite reading. "Yes, you could be right. If she bought 'em new—and I reckon she did—she's got a lot of mileage out of them."

Stone nodded. "I've no strong objections to secondhand books myself—beggarly students can't be choosers—but the Summers family don't seem the type to frequent charity shops and jumble sales, somehow." She smiled. "Unless it was one of her famous Rebellious Gestures, of course."

"Check in the wardrobe," suggested Trewley. "My three often come back with odds and ends they've picked up in Oxfam, and so long as it's washable I can't say it bothers us too much. Teaches 'em to manage their pocket money. . . ."

He recalled Alison's words on the financial learning habits of the young and fell into an awkward silence. His sergeant cleared her throat and hurried across to obey his courteous command.

The wardrobe door was locked: and the key, unusually, was not in the lock. It took several minutes' search before Stone found it at the bottom of the drawer in which Claire kept her underwear. "Still split," observed the sergeant, holding up what were clearly the St. Catherine's regulation Aertex knickers beside a wispy confection of lace and not much else. "Well, nobody knows at that age what sort of person they're going to turn into. . . ."

She turned the key in the lock and pulled the door open. She whistled softly. "Not much of *this* came from Oxfam, if I'm any judge. Gosh, I must be way out of touch with the pocket money habits of today's youth if they can afford this sort of gear. . . ."

"More money than sense," growled Trewley. "The parents, I mean." He frowned. "Only one of them earning. He must have a pretty high-powered job."

"That's why she didn't want us to fish him out of his precious meeting," Stone reminded him rather waspishly. "The higher the power, the higher the price—the company," she enlarged as Trewley blinked at her. "You know what these firms are like, sir. They've bought Richard Summers, body and soul."

"Umph," said Trewley, who had taken the Queen's Shilling—or the constabulary equivalent—and been proud to do so for what many might call a minimal wage. "Well paid or not, it sounds as if he kept a tight rein on the girls.

Tried to, at any rate. Nose to the grindstone: not even a Saturday job . . ."

There followed a meditative pause, which the superintendent eventually broke by voicing the now obvious thought. "I wonder if young Claire hasn't got some . . . other source of money nobody knows about?"

"Blackmail." Stone had been leafing through the scrapbook she had discovered on the wardrobe shelf. "She's a good-looking girl, sir. A bit . . . flamboyant, perhaps—"

"You mean tarty." Trewley was looking over her shoulder at the *Argus* cuttings of Claire's success as Desdemona, and the costume photographs taken to a near-professional standard by, he supposed, the school photographer, for publicity purposes. "I'm not much of a one for culture, Stone, but as I remember it, the wife was framed by a bloke who was peeved he didn't make two-eye-see." Stone smiled inwardly at this summary of Iago's failed career as Othello's second in command. "Good actress the girl may be," he went on, "but she looks far too . . . chirpy in all these snaps. Pleased with herself, which isn't what I'd've expected if you'd asked me. I'd've expected her to look miserable rather than chirpy, with her husband accusing her of what-have-you with all and sundry all over the show. Wouldn't you?"

"The miserable ones might come later. . . ." Stone went on turning pages. "Only they don't. Well, perhaps she felt looking miserable didn't, um, do her justice." Stone was, after all, female; and closer in years to the youthful Claire than Trewley had been for several decades. "Your appearance matters dreadfully at that age. Mind you, I would have thought that for a theatrical portfolio to show agents, she ought really to have proved she could do more than look glamorous. . . ."

"Perhaps she couldn't." Claire Summers was certainly an attractive—much more than attractive—girl. But there was, behind the undoubted attraction, something . . . hard about her. . . . "Perhaps that's why her father didn't want her trying for the stage. He knew she didn't have the brains, or the sticking-power, to make the most of what was probably a flash in the pan—not in an acceptable, respect-able way, I mean." He rubbed his chin as he contemplated the first portrait of Claire, to which Stone had returned. "If that's a good likeness, it'll do for us to give out—but there's a definite look of the casting-room couch in that expression, wouldn't you say?"

Stone studied the perfect cheekbones, the inscrutable eyes, and the unspoken promise in the half-parted lips. "Now you mention it, sir . . ."

"We've still that diary to find." Trewley began opening drawers, pulling them three-quarters of the way out, groping underneath for anything taped to the underside, tapping the back for any less hollow sound that might indicate an alien presence, feeling carefully among and between the folded garments for anything unusual. "If we're right, and she's been getting money to live the high life from some poor devil she's kept dangling—one way or another—she'll have kept some sort of record of what he paid." He shook his head. "Pity it's an all-girls school. A teacher would've been the obvious target. . . ."

Stone did not make the obvious remark. There were some matters on which the superintendent preferred to follow the orthodox line for as long as possible.

The bulldog gloom lightened. "But there's always the neighbours. Family friends. Maybe extra maths coaching, an outside drama teacher, something of that sort. We'll check with Mrs. Summers after we've done here—and in young Emma's room, too."

The bulldog sighed. "Emma's savings book is with her father, Mrs. Summers said. Odds are Claire's is, too—but at that age, they're after a sight more . . . freedom. Privacy." Stone, busily hunting through the pockets of Claire's several jackets, dresses, and skirts, still said nothing. "She'll have her secrets hidden away. Stone—and nowhere too difficult, either. At that age, they know it all. They think they can get away with anything they like because they're so much smarter than the fool adults they have to deal with. They'd never dream anyone older would be able to—ah!"

"Do you mean, 'Aha,' sir?" Stone had paused in her hunt, with one hand holding the next item to be searched. "As in the sense of 'Eureka!'?"

"I've found it," agreed Trewley. "At least, I've found *something*." Even at such a time, he managed a faint rumble of what in a less lugubrious individual might have been amusement. "Though I don't propose to rush out of here and up the road shouting about it starkers until I know just what it is young madam thinks is worth keeping hidden under the lining paper. . . ."

He balanced the bottom-but-one drawer of the bedside chest on one large hand, while with the other he rummaged under the close-packed piles of T-shirts and light woollen sweaters. Stone heard the rustle of paper, the scrabble of fingers, and a slight tearing sound, followed immediately by an oath.

"Well, well." The hand emerged clutching its prize, and the drawer was slipped shut again. "Well, well, well. What do you make of this, Stone? As a medical type, I mean."

And the superintendent held out to his sergeant a half-used packet of contraceptive pills.

──────── Nineteen ────────

"No," ALISON INSISTED for the third time. Trewley had sent Stone to question Claire's mother while he began the search of Emma's room. "She didn't—doesn't—have a boyfriend. Richard—I mean, we both think that at sixteen she should be concentrating on her studies."

It was a fine theory—but theory and practice, the sergeant knew, were two very different things where teenage girls were concerned. Especially teenage girls with old-fashioned fathers, ineffectual mothers, and developing wills of their own . . .

Stone said gently: "Does she have any . . . female problems?" There were often good medical reasons for prescribing the pill. It seemed unlikely in Claire's case—why take so much trouble to conceal something about which her mother must have known?—but the girl had to be given the benefit of the doubt. . . .

Doubt dispelled. Firmly Alison was shaking her head. "She's one of the healthiest children for miles. It was always Emma who caught whatever bugs were going around."

Her voice cracked; her face crumpled. "Oh! Emma . . ."

Stone patted her on the shoulder, murmured soothingly, and left her. She must help her superior in his search. They had found nothing, apart from the pills, out of the ordinary in Claire's room. Alison's answers to the sergeant's pocket-money query might imply an outside source of income, but there had been no definite proof. It had been Trewley, wise in the ways of family life, who suggested that the elder girl, in a classic double-bluff, might have hidden her most secret secrets in a place no prying younger sister—or parent—would ever dream of looking.

"Not to mention Emma could've kept a diary too," he added, before dismissing Stone to her questioning of Alison. "If there's anything to find, we'll find it. . . ."

From the self-indulgence of Claire's room to the strict discipline of Emma's was more than a mere four years' distance. Stone paused on the threshold, looking about her. The same faint chime that had echoed earlier—which had been for a time silenced by the discovery of Emma's body—now sounded again in her mind.

She tested it out loud. She coughed. "What do you make of her books, sir?"

Trewley was replacing the last one on the shelf. He had shaken each in turn, in case any was hollow—an out-dated smugglers' trick which the suspicions he, like Stone, had begun to harbour about Emma had suggested she might employ.

She hadn't. "Nothing," he said. "In one sense." He favoured his sergeant with a knowing look.

She looked as knowingly back at him. "But in another sense?" she prompted as a good sidekick should. "The, um, subject matter, maybe?"

"Every Agatha Christie ever published, I should think, plus a whole load of folk I've never heard of, but they all look out of the same mould. Library books the same, though I do recognise a couple of 'em from the telly."

He was working towards the same solution: it was logical, really. "A camera for her birthday," reflected Stone, and saw his approving nod. "Photos of people—strangers. Ditto tyre tracks and footprints. Likes to dress up—disguise. Wanting—no, *needing* a black jacket . . ."

"It all fits, doesn't it?" Trewley sighed. "The poor little brat was a loner. Overshadowed by her sister, no close friends—and a sight too much imagination for her own good. She wanted to make something of herself—wanted to be important in her own eyes, at least. She wanted to do it properly. . . ."

"She wanted to be a private detective," supplied Stone, sighing in her turn. "Down these mean streets," she quoted sadly. "And I have the most awful feeling that for Emma they . . . well, *were* mean, in the worst possible sense. My guess is she went out detecting, and quite by chance stumbled on something—"

"And followed it up." Trewley was more interested in deduction than in good manners. "A kid her age wouldn't go prowling out of the house in the middle of the night without a damn good reason—"

"And she wouldn't know there *was* a reason unless she'd seen something suspicious at a . . . at what would be a more normal time for, um, a kid her age. And then . . ."

Once again they looked at each other in knowing fashion. Both sighed for the tragedy of it all.

"She'll have given it some highfaluting name like a—a case book," Trewley said at last in bracing accents. "Or a log, or a dossier—but it'll be her diary, Stone, whatever she called it. And we've got to find it. . . ."

Emma Summers had been slightly more ingenious than the professional searchers had given her credit for. They drew a blank in the bedside chest of drawers, under the mattress, and inside the zip-fastened cover of a lumpy cushion on her writing chair. It was Stone's sharper eyes that noticed how the side edge of the padded bedhead facing away from the window, and thus in permanent shade, had a finish less neat than the top and the other, illuminated, side.

She pulled gently at the fabric with her fingers. With no sound of tearing, it parted company from the wall . . . to reveal a hollow, deliberately carved, in the thick foam against which Emma's pillows rested . . .

And inside that carved-out hollow was a notebook with dark green covers and a spiral binding.

"She started it back in the autumn, sir."

"New school," said Trewley. "Unsettling."

Stone nodded as she scanned the first few entries. "The sort of thing you'd expect at the beginning. She wants to keep a record of her experiences for use in later life. . . ." She cleared her throat. "Seems she had visions of being a writer and thought it would be valuable material, sir."

Trewley grunted. After a pause Stone continued.

"She doesn't find it easy to make friends. . . . Claire and *her* friends tease her. . . . Some of the teachers make her nervous—not in the sense of being scared, though. I don't think there's anything for us in that. . . . Some lessons are more difficult than she would like to admit, but her parents don't seem to understand why she's worrying. If Claire didn't have problems at the same age, why should Emma . . ."

"That," said Trewley, "is an argument we've never been daft enough to use with any of our three. For heaven's sake, everybody's different. Poor little kid . . ."

Stone was leafing through the pages more quickly now. "She's interested in the footpath protesters—wonders if it's all part of some Conspiracy against the school on the part of an Enemy." She looked up, smiling at memories of her own youthful self. "She's overdosed on Angela Brazil and Enid Blyton, and all those High Jinks in the Dorm, Rivals of the Fourth stories, I should think."

"Nothing but detective yarns on the shelves now," the superintendent reminded her, rubbing his chin. "New. Mrs. Summers said Emma asked her to give all her toys to charity. Books count as toys, I imagine—and then, she didn't give them, so we can always check."

"If we've guessed right about the private eye business, the footpath and the theatre project seem to be what set her off," Stone said after a few minutes more. "She's stopped worrying about conspiracies now, but she wants to know who and what and why, in case it's all a cover-up for something more sinister. . . ."

Trewley snorted. "Sinister? A bunch of anoraks waving

banners, and half a dozen middle-class grannies who used to climb the trees when *they* were Katies? Besides, the theatre was moved from the original site which annoyed 'em so much—*and* they rerouted the path, to show willing. And it worked. Calmed down nicely, everyone did."

"Yes, sir, but at that age you don't easily let go of an idea once it's taken your fancy. I'm sure Emma wanted to be a heroine and, um, Unmask the Traitors. And when there were no—no obvious traitors, she decided to start looking for them, in a more methodical way than just watching them stand in picket lines shouting slogans at men on bulldozers."

"But that's all they were doing," objected Trewley. "When that theatre was opened, we hardly heard a peep out of them—and we've heard nothing since. They stopped making waves once the school agreed to compromise. I refuse to believe there was anything anyone was doing, apart from protesting, that would lead 'em to—to murder a child who took a bit more interest in 'em than they thought healthy. Dammit, Stone, it's not as if they were a bunch of Rent-a-Mob yahoos brought in by bus from heaven knows where. They were locals, the lot of them."

Stone observed that Allingham people were no more—or less—criminally inclined than their country cousins.

Trewley snorted. "You don't have to tell me that. But whatever it was—*if* it was—there hasn't been a sniff of it. And if there's been anything wrong—so wrong a schoolkid could spot it—then you'd think someone a bit more . . . experienced would have noticed *something*, after—how long? Six months?"

"Perhaps," said Stone, "it took six months to plan."

"And young Emma followed it right the way along?"

There was a lengthy pause. "If she did," said Stone, having scanned another fortnight's entries, "she didn't put anything down. You're probably right, sir. What happened to Emma has nothing to do with the protesters. But—"

"We can't be sure," he supplied. "We'll have 'em checked

out, just in case. Still, I can't see that theatre's got anything to do with her death, not really. . . ."

"Apart from the fact that Claire was the star of the first production." Another entry had caught Stone's eye. "Talk about Emma's nose out of joint—she auditioned with the rest of her class and didn't even get to carry a spear, poor child."

"And her big sister landed the plum." Trewley sighed. "What do they call it—sibling rivalry? I believe them."

"She was madly jealous, as well as thoroughly miserable. I'm not in the least surprised." Stone turned another page. "And the longer it goes on, and once the family rows begin, the more jealous and miserable she starts to feel. And now she blames it all on Claire. . . ."

"It isn't Claire who's dead," said Trewley, who knew how high adolescent passions could run. "Not that the kid would have done more than daydream about getting rid of Big Sister—who has certainly disappeared," he added as Stone read on without replying. "There's *got* to be a connection. . . ."

"This could be it, sir." Stone spoke quickly. "From thinking about sleuthing unnamed conspirators, she's decided it's Claire who ought to be sleuthed. If there's anything she's up to that will make her less of everyone's blue-eyed girl, Emma wants to find it." She looked at Trewley, who was scowling. "How much do you bet me she did?"

"Umph." He scowled still more. "You don't catch me that way. Does she give any idea of what she might or might not have found out?"

A silence, broken only by the rhythmic rustle of paper. "Not until after they'd finished with *Othello*." She sighed. "Emma must have been terribly wretched for her to have gone on writing—thinking—feeling this way for so long. You wonder her parents didn't notice something was the matter. . . . Or perhaps you don't," she added as the superintendent snorted with even more vehemence than usual. "If they were totally wrapped up in Claire . . ."

"As was Emma." A further rustling, rhythmic silence. "With very good reason!" And now there was a note of triumph in her voice.

"Let me see." Trewley shot out an eager hand to seize the green-covered diary, then remembered, shook his head, and subsided, muttering. "Damned spider-tracks. Read it to me, will you?"

It had been only when he admitted, many months after her arrival, that his close eyesight wasn't as comfortable as in his younger days that Stone felt herself fully accepted as a member of the superintendent's team. He never spelled it out in words, of course: but it was mutually understood that he found her presence tolerable, and occasionally helpful; and it was mutually agreed that where there was reading to be done away from the police station, when the Trewley spectacles—which he seldom wore—were conspicuous by their even more marked absence, then it was Stone who did it.

"Listen, sir. 'I am surer than ever C. has a boyfriend. He must have lots of money, because I have picked the lock of her wardrobe and seen the lovely clothes he has bought her. I taught myself how to do this from *Strong Poison*.' That," she interposed hastily, as the superintendent's mouth opened in a horrified grimace, "is a famous detective story from the 1930s, I believe."

He mopped his brow. "Yes, well, I *was* wondering. The poor kid was stabbed, as far as we know, not poisoned. One electrocuted, one strangled, and young Emma—oh, God!"

Stone watched his face turn purple, then pale. "Are you all right, sir? You look ghastly."

"I feel it." He closed his eyes and groaned. "Suppose for all my fine words earlier we *have* got a random killer—a maniac—to deal with? Isn't that the sort of thing they were always doing in Agatha Christie?" He opened his eyes to glare at Stone, who had gasped in horrified protest. "Mark my words, he'll drown the next one in that pond of theirs, and try a—a blunt instrument for the next, a branch from one of those blasted trees or something—and then a shotgun, or a—"

"Don't!" begged his sergeant, in two minds whether to laugh or shudder. "This is—this is real life, sir, not a detective story. Whoever he is, he's not mad. He has his own logical reasons for killing three people, and if we only knew what they were . . ."

"Three females." It was not a response to her final observation. "Assorted ages, but all of 'em connected, one way or another, with St. Catherine's—and a fourth female missing, Stone." The flight of fancy was abruptly grounded. "What d'you reckon—run off to the boyfriend? Does young Emma give us any clues?"

"Um. 'I think C. must meet him at night. Nobody in Sing Sing has ever reported her to the Dragons for playing truant, and I am sure someone would notice if she did.' Sing Sing for the school, I suppose, and her parents will be the Dragons."

Trewley didn't dispute this guess, but nodded for her to continue. She coughed. "'I have followed Subject C. twice on different Saturdays, but she only went to the record shop and the ironmonger, and to the café to have coffee with her stupid friends. I don't think she saw me, so she probably wasn't laying a false trail. But sometimes she is tired in the mornings, and the Dragons send both of us, even their precious C., to bed early in term time. Nobody is sleeping well this hot weather, but she is more tired than that, and she has a soppy look on her face sometimes. Our windows are always open. If I wanted to climb out, I know I could, and if C. didn't always pretend to be so grown up, I know she could, too.'"

Stone stopped reading and shook her head. "It's a romantic idea, having to do a Juliet-from-the-balcony to meet your boyfriend, but I somehow can't see one of today's more, um, rational teenagers shinning down a drainpipe for a spot of togetherness. Can you, sir?"

"Well, my three've got more sense." Trewley paused. "I hope. But as to whether Miss Claire's a sensible girl . . ."

"She's on the pill, which is more than some of the silly creatures think of doing."

"Umph." Trewley shuddered. This conversation was more than uncomfortable for a man in his domestic situation. "It could all just be Emma's imagination, of course. . . ."

"You don't go on the pill for fun," said Stone, medical expert. "What other reason than a boyfriend would she have? That her mother doesn't know about, I mean. And if we're going to believe what Emma says, then I think I can guess how . . . Yes." She found the place, marked it with a finger, and prepared to explain.

"Think about it, sir. You're positively bursting with souped-up hormones, and so is your boyfriend." The father of three could only groan. Stone hurried on: "Agreed, you might just about climb *down* a drainpipe, or a—a knotted sheet, or something. But it isn't going to be that easy to climb back up again, especially if you're worn out from a passionate bout of hanky-panky. Is it?"

The superintendent growled something about his sergeant having hidden depths and knowing rather more than he thought decent, for a girl like her.

"Think about shipwrecked sailors," said Stone at once.

The bulldog boggled. "Look here, Stone, if this hot weather's turned your head at last, then—"

"No, sir, cross my heart, this is absolutely genuine. When rescue ships drop scrambling nets over the side, it's the sailors who climb to the top who are far more likely to die than those who just hang on until someone hauls them up. They're all physically weak from trying not to drown, but they don't realise it while the water keeps them afloat. The shock to the system of suddenly having all that extra weight to haul vertically up the net does their hearts no good at all. And I know," she said as he began to splutter, "you'll say

Claire hasn't been frolicking in a swimming pool—as far as we know—but the same principle applies, surely? She'd want the easy way back. Anyone would."

"Fair enough," he said after a pause. "So what's your theory of how she managed it? If she did," he added from force of pessimistic habit.

She consulted the diary. "Emma followed her sister, who went to the coffee place and the record shop—*and to the ironmongers.*" Trewley uttered a growl, but she gave him no time to say more. "It isn't the shoe-repair place, sir, I know—but if they don't cut spare keys, too, then I'll be very much surprised. Don't you agree?"

And he could find no fault with her argument.

Twenty

EMMA'S DIARY YIELDED few further clues. The last-but-final entry made a reference to the younger sister's resolve to stay awake and follow Claire next time she went out; the last entry of all said that the previous night's storm had forced a twenty-four-hour delay on the young detective—and on her quarry.

"'It is silly,'" read Stone aloud, "'for a private eye to be scared of thunder. I am sure Hercule Poirot and Philip Marlowe are not.'" She coughed. "No comment, sir." Trewley said nothing. She went on: "'But I know Subject C. is scared, too. If she does go out tonight, I don't think she will go far, in case the storm comes back. The forecast says there is a possibility.'"

Trewley sighed. "And we have to assume she did. They did. Claire going out to meet . . . whoever, and Emma doing her turned-up-collar behind-the-bushes routine, poor kid. Somewhere along the line, Claire gets away from her, and while she's wandering about trying to pick up the trail, she bumps into . . . Chummie."

"The boyfriend, do you think?"

"Who knows?" He lumbered to his feet. "Bring the diary with you. We won't waste any more time here, Stone. If Mrs. Summers has no idea who the boyfriend is—where Claire might have gone—then her pals at school might know. And we're going to get it out of them. . . ."

• • •

THEY DIDN'T. NEITHER the comradely skill of fellow female Sergeant Stone, nor the fatherly approach—bluff and gently bullying by turns—of Superintendent Trewley could wring from Claire's closest friends the information the detectives had, in the end, to be convinced the girls did not possess. All that could be done was to arrange for copies of Claire's photograph to be printed and distributed in the appropriate manner, before Trewley and Stone abandoned their questioning and returned to the scene of the latest crime.

In a brooding silence they contemplated the now empty shrubbery. Trewley dabbed the back of his neck with his handkerchief. Stone pushed a lock of dark hair off her sunwarmed face and sighed.

"Sir!" The thump of regulation boots, growing louder as the wearer approached. "Mr. Trewley, sir!"

It was PC Benson, buttons agleam with the importance of his message. "Sergeant Pleate's radioed in, sir."

Trewley swallowed an automatic curse. He knew the desk sergeant would not prosecute a professional squabble in the middle of a murder investigation. "Doc Watson's done his preliminary report," said Benson, once he was close enough to thwart potential eavesdroppers. "She was stabbed all right—but with two different instruments, before and after death. And she was moved in between, sir, too."

Trewley didn't bother to ask how the doctor could be so sure. Such matters as postmortem lividity and bleeding, or lack of it, were routine forensic knowledge even for old-fashioned coppers like himself, coppers who preferred feel, and instinct based on past experience, to hard scientific facts that were sometimes no more than so much jargon.

"Did he have any idea about weapons?"

"Ordinary knife, for the actual killing." Benson consulted his notebook. "Probably the folding pocket type, with a blade about six inches long. There are bruises round the throat as if he tried shaking her first to keep her quiet, and one big bruise on the side of her face as if he'd slapped her silly before shoving the knife in her ribs, the doc thinks."

Stone shuddered. Trewley grunted. Emma Summers had been just twelve years old, and small for her age. The picture painted by Benson's words were very bleak.

"Right in the heart, poor kiddie," said Benson. "Then she was left somewhere for an hour or so; then he moved her here." He glanced up from his notes to indicate the tangle of low-growing bushes by the wall of the needlework room. "The second weapon . . . that's a bit of a mystery, doc says. She was stabbed—well, more like slashed—in the throat, but odds are it wouldn't have killed her. If the knife hadn't got her first, I mean." Benson, a young man not much given to flowery speech, gazed warily at his superior before adding:

"It's almost as if he was . . . being symbolic, Doc says. Making a gesture, sir," he added in haste as the superintendent let forth a furious snort.

"A maniac. I knew it," muttered Trewley. At his side Stone stirred.

"Very short blade, no more than half an inch," went on Benson, having waited in vain for the sergeant to speak. "Slightly curved. Very sharp along the business edge, but, uh, thicker along the, uh, opposite side. Sort of out of proportion for a knife, he said—and this is the really odd bit. He says there are these funny little round bruises with every cut. Sort of . . . matching. Just as if it had a—a sort of little lump at the back."

The constable's honest face registered sudden sympathy for the perplexed and exasperated expression on the face of his superior. He coughed. "Doc's faxed a likely drawing to the station, sir, but of course Sergeant Pleate wasn't able to—"

Exasperation turned to a near explosion, and Benson shut up with remarkable promptitude.

Stone hurried into the breach. "What exactly is the—are

the necks wounds like? Neat or ragged?" She gulped. "One quick stab, or a—or a messy slash?"

Trewley's personal TNT level sank to its normal "simmer" as he regarded his sergeant in surprise. It was well known around the station that she didn't like anything too gory. Didn't even like thinking about it; certainly not talking about it. Yet here she was, asking questions—and not just to stop him blowing his top at young Benson, he'd risk a sizeable bet. She had that look about her that said she'd got an idea and wanted to try it out. . . .

Benson shrugged. "Well . . . queer, Sarge. He says he's never seen anything like it before. Sort of jagged ripping, he says. Like—like tearing with hiccups, if you see what I mean."

Stone shivered. "I think . . . maybe I do." She paused, as both men stared for the peculiar certainty of her tone. "I think." She paused again. She made up her mind. "Look, I know it sounds crazy, but . . ."

"I said he was a maniac." Trewley knew he was stating the obvious. It wasn't like Stone to dither and haver this way when she had an idea: but he could hardly bawl her out in front of Benson. "I *said* he was a maniac. Well, what's the medical expert's view of his particular mania?"

She didn't blush. "I'm no expert in mental illness, sir—but I think the doctor could be right about a—a gesture. If the weapon is . . . what I've guessed, there can't possibly be any other reason for a sane person to . . . I mean, you could hardly kill anyone outright. . . . And, gesture or not, it's quite . . . horrible. Sick." She ignored the look of perplexed exasperation that had returned to the superintendent's face. "I think the killer is trying, for whatever reason—whether he's a genuine maniac or just trying to be too clever—to make us notice . . ." She took a deep breath. "To make us notice the link with the needlework room."

"The *what?*"

"Yes, sir." Now she'd brought it out at last, it didn't seem so difficult to continue. "Just think a moment. Mrs. Tanner was electrocuted in that room by a sewing machine. Mrs. French was strangled there by the belt from a treadle. And Emma was brought as close as possible . . ."

"Hidden," interjected Trewley.

"Delaying tactics, sir. To confuse us about the time of death—but the sewing connection is still valid, I think." She coughed. "And what else I think is that if Doc Watson studies the wounds of Emma's neck carefully, he'll find they were inflicted by somebody using a . . ." Her distaste for the idea was very apparent. "A stitch ripper, sir. Ugh." And she shivered again.

Benson, blessed with four older sisters and a domesticated mother, after a brief pause for puzzling gave congratulatory tongue. "Hey, that's right! Well done, Sarge!"

"Why?" demanded Trewley, who never resented it when his subordinates knew more than he did, but who hated being kept in the dark once they'd worked out something that still had him stumped. "A stitch ripper, you say? Some gadget for needlework, I suppose."

Benson knew his place. He kept quiet and let Stone do the explaining.

"Yes, sir. They're special little tools for unpicking where you've gone wrong." Despite the gravity of the situation, a rueful grin curved her lips and mirrored the droll memories sparkling in her eyes. "Tiny knives—just four or five inches long, I suppose, but more than half handle, and the blade itself less than an inch—and curved, sir. And with another, blunted blade-type piece over the top like a hook, with a bobble on the end to stop the material slipping out of control . . ."

The constable was nodding; the superintendent was scowling. Suddenly he chuckled. "Benson, for pity's sake lend her your notebook. A bobble on the end!"

"Here you are, Sarge. And a pencil."

"Thanks." She turned carefully to a clean page and shook her head. "It's ages since I did any sewing, but . . .

something like this, I think . . ." And Benson's notebook was presented for inspection.

"Umph." Trewley frowned as he studied Stone's basic, but informative, sketch. "When my wife sews—which isn't that often, so I might've forgotten—and it goes wrong, I think she uses special scissors for unpicking." With his free hand he described a curious shape in the air. "Little oblong snippy things, with an extra bit for her thumb. I'm not sure I've seen one of these rippers before."

Benson was brooding; Stone got there first. "Oh, yes—I know what you're describing, sir. Snippers are a more versatile tool, which is probably why they're more popular, even though they're more expensive. Better value for money, you see. You can snip fabric as well as stitches, whereas all you can really do with a stitch ripper . . ."

She realised what she'd said, and promptly subsided.

Benson shuffled now from one large foot to the other, giving every appearance of being great with theory but reluctant to speak. Trewley, still pondering the idea of the stitch ripper Needlework Gesture, glowered as he mopped his face with his handkerchief. "Ants in your pants, lad?"

"Sorry, sir."

"You're young." It was undeniable. "You can cope with this heat a damn sight better than me, so it can't be that. For heaven's sake, spit it out if you've got something to say. I won't eat you."

Benson shot a quick look at Stone, who winked. He found himself grinning back. "It's—it's the stitch ripper, sir. Begging your pardon, Sarge, because I bet you're right about what it is, but—if he wanted to make that sort of . . . uh, gesture, why make such a blinking mystery of it? Who's to say anyone would ever have guessed? It's not exactly your common or garden weapon. I mean, so as to be *sure* we'd get the needlework bit, why not just stab her with a pair of scissors after the knife? You can't mistake scissors. Have the blades half open, say, and there isn't really much else they could be."

Stone, banishing reckless thoughts of snake bites, with a nod conceded this argument, and began to search for a way round it. Trewley, after a pause, grunted that the lad had a point. Benson stared ahead with resolution. Stone, after a pause of her own, chuckled.

So, after yet another pause, did Trewley.

The sergeant sobered first. "*If* he wanted to emphasise the needlework side—well, a hairdresser or a florist or—or practically anyone else uses scissors. There's nothing special about them for sewing." Memories of her schooldays returned. "Unless they're pinking shears, of course, though I imagine those would be quite hard to stab anyone with . . ."

"And messy," added Benson as Stone made a face.

"Oh?" The face of the superintendent had assumed a frown of half-remembered doubt.

Stone recovered herself. "Yes, sir. Pinking shears are those strong scissors with zigzag blades for cutting, um, zigzag lines to stop raw edges fraying. But Benson's right. It would make a perfectly horrible mess."

"Then maybe he *isn't* 'he,' after all," Trewley said as his sergeant grimaced again. "Maybe a woman wouldn't want that sort of . . . uh, mess to deal with, let alone dispose of the weapon once she'd done the job. This ripper thing's . . . what, five inches long? Easy to slip down a drain, or chuck in the pond, or dig a hole and bury it. Full-size scissors, on the other hand . . ."

"And, if she—or he—pinched the ripper from in there," suggested Stone, with a nod for the windows of the nearby needlework room, "it's obvious a pair of scissors or shears gone missing would be noticed far more quickly than the disappearance of something so much smaller, and cheaper. She—or he—knew Emma would be found eventually, but the later the better, of course."

"Trying to confuse us over the time of death?" Trewley rubbed his chin and sighed. "If anyone had presented us with an alibi, I'd feel happier about accepting that part of your argument, Sergeant—but they haven't. Still, the rest of it makes some kind of sense." He sighed again. "But . . . what kind? Maybe we're reading too much into it, and it's all some blasted red herring. And if he or she *is* making a gesture, what does it mean? The killer's got to be an odd sort to be driven mad by needlework. . . ."

"The oddest things," his sergeant reminded him gently, "drive people crazy in weather like this, sir."

"Umph." Trewley resumed his study of the pencilled Stitch Ripper. "More than crazy. This doesn't look the sort of thing anyone would carry about in a pocket on the off chance, maniac or otherwise. Forget it was there and sit down suddenly, and you could give yourself a nasty jab."

"Oh!" Stone waved the pencil in an apologetic manner. "They do sometimes come with a cap on the sharp end, but they soon get lost or broken. If it *was* pinched from the needlework room—well, with crowds of schoolgirls larking about the place, I'd lay you odds any little plastic cap would be both broken and lost within minutes."

Trewley couldn't argue with that. He said: "*If* that's where he got it. Or she. He's still more likely, but . . ."

"Yes, sir." Stone was thinking aloud. "Look, if we accept that all three murders were committed by the same person, with or without a sewing fixation, they've none of them required any great physical strength. And some women don't mind blood as much as, um, others. But a man would have far less reason to be carrying a stitch ripper around with him than a woman. . . ."

"Which makes it very obviously a woman's crime," supplied Trewley as she came to a halt. "Too obviously? Your average man mightn't have known about these zigzag shears of yours, but this ripper thing is so over-egging the pudding that—Benson, for heaven's sake!"

"Sorry, sir." He was shuffling again. "It's just . . . well, thinking about a woman. She'd need to be strong to've brought her here, wouldn't she? From where she killed her—not that I reckon it'll have been far, this weather."

Glumly the superintendent nodded. The grounds of St. Catherine's—distant tree-lined tennis courts and lawns, spinney and copse and pond in the greater distance—were undoubtedly spacious.

Benson plunged on. "Having to carry even a slip of a thing like young Emma a little way'd be a long way, if you know what I mean." Warily he looked at Stone. "For a man, let alone a woman." He took the plunge. "Er—could you have done it, Sarge?"

She pushed back her hair from her face as she considered the problem dispassionately. "If we're realistic, and discount the possibility of a killer so steeped in lunacy that she's mad with the strength of ten normal people . . . Well, I doubt if I could have carried Emma's body very far, and I'd say I'm both fitter, and stronger, than the average female my size. And age."

Trewley scowled. "And how many of the females we've interviewed are younger than you? Or in better nick, if they're older? We're back with 'he' again, blast it."

"No—wait, sir." Uniformed Benson was beginning to enjoy this plain-clothes detection lark. "How about a—a wheelbarrow?"

"A what?"

"No tracks." Benson waved expansively at the asphalt, brick, and gravel of playground and garden and path. "And that grass," he continued with a more expansive wave for the distant greensward. "I know it rained the other night, but with all those girls messing about playing games . . ."

He stopped. He blushed. "Sorry, sir, but remembering that was what made me think of it, you see."

"Think of *what?*" If there was an idea to be had in this confusing case, Trewley wanted it. Now.

"Sorry, sir." Benson blushed more deeply still. "But—well, like I said, with the tracks messed up we've no hope of finding if she came that way—and why should she? I'd take the quickest route, if it was me—though that wasn't what I meant, sir. It was . . ." He gulped. Perhaps being plainclothes wouldn't be so much fun, after all. "Er—it was the skipping, sir, sort of put it in my head, and . . ."

"Skipping?" Trewley stared. Benson was looking more hot and bothered than he'd ever seen him before. . . . *Hot.* Was the weather the answer? Had he got another madman to deal with, quite apart from a triple killer (whether male or female) wandering around uncaught? "The girl was stabbed to death with a six-inch knife, Constable, not savaged by a mountain goat."

He found himself glancing at Stone for guidance. From her response he would know if the lad was turning dangerous or not. . . .

Evidently not. Not unless the heat had got to her, too. She didn't look worried; she was nodding and smiling.

"Hey, that's right!" cried Sergeant Stone in complimentary echo. "Oh, well done, Benson. Sir, you must remember. With three daughters . . . Salt, mustard, vinegar, pepper. Coach, carriage, wheelbarrow, dustcart. This year, next year . . . *You* know, sir."

"Carriage? Don't remind me! He could've killed her miles off the school premises, for all we know, and brought her here by car." He glowered across the sunbaked grounds. "And then there's that damned public footpath running right through the place. . . ."

Stone grinned at Benson, who was looking deflated. "Or a bicycle," she suggested. Give her gloomy superior the worst case first, and he might just be more receptive to the (possibly) better . . . "A man's bike, of course. The body tied to the crossbar—well, perhaps not. Doc Watson would have mentioned rope burns. But Benson's had a brainwave, sir. You could certainly wheel a body in a barrow a lot farther than you could carry it, and there'd be no visible tracks on the path."

"Umph." He favoured Benson with a penetrating stare. "Well . . ."

"And," the sergeant pressed on, "the new theatre's not the only building the path runs past, sir. Nobody sensible would keep a wheelbarrow in a theatre—but suppose we were to check the groundsman's hut to see if anyone has been tampering with the lock?"

"Oh." There was a thoughtful silence. "Yes. Benson, maybe that's not such a bad idea. . . ." He rubbed his chin and scowled with the effort of ratiocination. "The groundsman's hut . . ."

There was another silence, during which his subordinates waited for him to lead the way.

He did not. He was still thinking.

He spoke.

"The groundsman," he said. "That Garner bloke. The one with the nervy wife . . ."

Twenty-one

"JULIE GARNER," SAID Stone thoughtfully. Benson, who had not been present at their previous encounters with the young woman in question, said nothing.

The sergeant considered her impressions of the unhappy helpmeet of the janitor-cum-groundsman. It must be no surprise that the announcement of murder, three times, within a quarter of a mile of home should make anyone unhappy: but poor Julie's general demeanour had hinted at a far greater strain than those fears any mother in a similar situation must suffer. With three small children, boisterous and forever squabbling; with herself pregnant—and not in the best of health—in a house of an awkward, old-fashioned design, Julie Garner's attempt to react in a normal manner during the three police interviews had been a gallant waste of effort that did not fool the professional interviewers. She was living on her nerves; was worn down by heat and an excess of domesticity. She needed help.

They knew this was not supplied by her husband. Julie had been too tired and wretched to suppress her routine complaints about Craig's growing neglect. Between bouts of yelling at the children to keep quiet, she grumbled about the still-broken video recorder, and how bored the kids were with just the telly, but there was no way *she* could fix it, though most things she could because if she didn't sort things out, nobody else would. She lamented the fact they lived so far from the public playground and didn't have a

car, because Craig had insisted they weren't to use any of
the school facilities even after hours, which didn't seem fair
when the place was so large they'd surely never be noticed.
All that room! All for the benefit of those stuck-up girls,
only there until four o'clock, swanking about in their posh
uniforms—and she shuddered to think what *they* cost, when
she was hard put to it to keep her three decently covered. . . .

"Sir!" Stone's eyes gleamed. "Remember? She makes
most of the children's clothes!"

Trewley nodded with slow satisfaction. "That's just what
I was thinking. Buys from the jumble and cuts the stuff to
size . . . and one of these stitch rippers'd cost a fair bit
less than a set of fancy snippers, with him only just back in
work and money still a bit tight . . ."

"The wife," ventured Benson, "would know where he
kept the keys to the wheelbarrow hut, sir. Wouldn't she?"

"She would." Trewley rubbed his chin and cast a suspicious glance upwards. "It's not that far for a walk," he said,
stifling a sigh. "She won't be going anywhere in a hurry,
this weather. We won't rush."

"Have we time to check the lock of the needlework room
first, sir?" Stone had seldom been so conscious that her
superior was growing no younger; or slimmer; or better able
to cope with the heat. How she would face Mrs. Trewley if
anything happened while the superintendent was in her
medical charge. . . . "To check the needlework room in
general, that is. It shouldn't take more than a few minutes,
with three of us. We ought to give Mrs. Garner the benefit
of the doubt about the stitch ripper until we're a little more
sure. . . ."

There were no immediate signs of tampering on the lock.

Benson began to observe that Mrs. Garner would also
know where her janitor husband kept the classroom keys,
but the superintendent's crime-prevention groan silenced
him.

Stone was contemplating the layout of benches and
tables. "Everything's been moved round," she said slowly.

"Yes, of course, Miss Thoday thought . . . And I'd forgotten," she added as Trewley groaned again. "Wasn't a lot of equipment taken over to the old block for the exam sitters?"

They might as well face facts. "You know, sir, things have been shifted about so much in here, I'm afraid that if half a dozen stitch rippers had been pinched, nobody would notice. Especially outsiders like us. We'll have to check the hut, after all."

"Nice while it lasted." As they made once more for the open air, Trewley cast a wistful look back at the high ceilings of the wide, cool corridor. "We won't rush there," he said again. "That poky cottage . . . You can understand why the poor woman might flip her lid. This heat—and those ghastly children . . ."

He paused to mop his face with his handkerchief, which pause gave Stone time to point out that she was no more sympathetic to disruptive juveniles than he. Probably less so, indeed, since he was used to it and she—well, wasn't.

"My three were never like that." The growl came almost automatically from the throat of the paternal bulldog. He was, however, a fair-minded man. "If we'd been strapped for cash, mind, and living so cramped, I wouldn't like to swear they'd have been little angels," he added. "But I agree with you. If we want to talk quietly to their mother, we don't stand much chance of—Hey! Benson!"

"Me, sir?"

"You, Constable. Stop trying to sneak off elsewhere in pursuance of enquiries. There's more than one way of being on duty, lad. Fond of children, are you?"

Benson shot the superintendent a reproachful look, but said nothing. He looked even more reproachfully at Stone, who was trying not to grin.

Trewley's look was all innocence. "Versatility, Benson, that's what I like to encourage in my officers. And Sergeant Stone'll be the first to tell you I'm not one for . . . for gender stereotyping, right?"

"Right, sir," said Stone, who could see what was coming. Benson, similarly afflicted with foresight, sighed.

"There are enough blokes running around checking statements and measuring footprints, Benson. They won't miss one—but the sergeant and I would. You'll come with us to this groundsman's hut, and then to the man's house to act as . . . as moral support to your superiors while they question a difficult suspect. Right?"

"Right, sir," said Benson and trudged off gloomily in his superiors' wake.

The public footpath that had caused so much agitation among the Allingham citizenry ran from one side of the St. Catherine's grounds to the other, linking two main roads otherwise separated by long stretches of high-quality housing either side of the school. Car owners did not object to taking the roundabout route from one road to the other; pedestrians and cyclists did, for the whole area was hilly.

The path, having been re-routed with Allingham's grudging consent on condition that it was resurfaced in asphalt, entered through a side gate in the front wall to curve its way discreetly past the lawns and flower beds, the gravel and flagstones of the school's central complex. It branched off in the direction of the swimming pool and tennis courts, its main stem curving away once more between tall, stately trees past the new theatre to branch again towards the flat-roofed concrete hut in which was stored all the paraphernalia of the groundsman's craft.

"Yes. Well." Superintendent Trewley planted himself four-square in front of the door, and fixed the battered padlock with an accusing glare. "How could *anyone* know if *that*'d been tampered with? There's more damage there than in a week's worth of motorway prangs. Tampered with? Ha!" And he gave himself up to brooding on what he knew of Craig Garner's predecessor, an ebullient individual who had, after several warnings, been forced into early retirement when found drunk in charge of a petrol-driven lawn mower, giving the verge of the dual carriageway a trim it did not need. Anyone so cavalier in the matter of agricultural machinery would be just as careless where the insertion of keys into keyholes was concerned.

So brooded Trewley. Stone disregarded him with just the right amount of courtesy, slipping past him to examine the screws that held the padlock hasp on one side to the door, on the other side to its frame. Benson, another brooding presence, tramped off around the back of the hut, where it was cooler, and was gone for some time.

"No recent scratches," reported Stone, "and no signs of oil. I'd say nobody's been picking this lock—or, if they have, they've been both inefficient and unsuccessful."

"Thank you." The superintendent did not sound particularly grateful. "Where the hell's young Benson got to?"

His voice, irritably raised, had its effect. Benson appeared round the other corner, having completed his careful circumambulation. "No windows broken, sir." He looked modestly at his boots. "Er—no sign of anyone slipping a crowbar under the roof, either."

"Good grief!" Trewley regarded him with some awe. "Benson, you've got a criminal mind. Never in a month of Sundays would I have dreamed of levering off a flat roof to get at what was inside . . . probably," he added, "because I know they're usually bolted on." The youngster shouldn't be encouraged to grow smug. "Granted, it might be worth a try for something small—but this is a wheelbarrow we're talking about, remember? He'd have to be pretty desperate to go to those lengths to get it out of there—and strong, too. The roof must weigh a fair bit, and the walls are a good six foot. If a bloke's that strong, he won't need a barrow in the first place. He can carry the girl all the way there by himself—or with someone else, of course, though the same would still apply. Levers! Locks!"

In a better humour than he had been for many hours, the superintendent hustled his little team back down the path to yet another asphalt branch, which led to the house of Craig and Julie Garner.

None of the constabulary three was aware that their inspection of the groundsman's hut had been, from a distance, observed by a figure that chose to remain itself unobserved as they left the hut, and moved steadily Garnerwards. . . .

THEY COULD HEAR squeals and screams and high-pitched yells long before they reached the janitor's cottage. To inexpert ears it sounded as if a miniature massacre was under way, but Trewley assured his youthful henchpersons that the children were just playing.

"In the garden," he guessed. "Which means the two of us'll be able to go indoors for a nice quiet chat with their mother—while you, Benson, keep the little blighters from getting under our feet. All right?"

"If you say so, sir." The thoughts of Police Constable Benson, as he heard the muted laughter of Detective Sergeant Stone, were decidedly ambivalent.

"Front door's open." Stone spoke in a low voice, for she had no idea where Julie might be. "Odd, isn't it? With a triple killer wandering about, you'd think she'd be worried he might turn up here. . . ."

Unless the killer is here already: but there was no real need for her to add this aloud.

"Constable, you go round the back. Sergeant, do the honours here, please." Trewley—whose pace from the hut to the cottage had hardly been brisk—gave his forehead one final polka-dot mop before beginning what might well prove to be the definitive interview.

Benson squared his shoulders, sketched a salute, and marched grimly off to face the infant firing squad. Stone rapped on the knocker and waited.

She rapped again. She glanced at the superintendent, who scowled. She raised her voice.

"Mrs. Garner, are you there? May we come in?"
Silence.
It lasted fifteen seconds before Stone rapped for a third

time, more loudly than before. "Mrs. Garner, this is the police. We'd appreciate a few words with you. . . ."

Trewley was on the point of suggesting they should risk a charge of Unlawful Entry when a querulous voice addressed them from one of the upper windows. "What do you want this time? I'm not so good today. I was in the bathroom when you started bashing the place to bits. Can't you leave a girl in peace for a change?"

Trewley took over. "I'm afraid not, Mrs. Garner. We do need to talk to you. If you're feeling ill—well, my sergeant has medical training. May we come in?"

A further, resentful, silence. At last: "If I throw up all over you, don't say I didn't warn you. . . ."

The two detectives took this as an invitation to enter. Stone went first. If the poor woman really was ill, they wanted no accusation of delayed treatment to be cast at the police at any later stage.

"What's happened to the kids?" Julie, panting from her downstairs sprint, her face a sickly green, glanced from Trewley to Stone and back again. "Where are they? I can't hear them. Are you saying there's summat wrong? Has that murdering devil taken them? If they've been hurt, I—"

"Mrs. Garner, no!" The bulldog had to roar to make himself heard. "They're fine, believe me. They're safe in the garden. Another of my officers is keeping them amused"—he'd almost said *under control*—"while we talk."

Even as he tried to explain, Trewley began to wonder if the proposed talk would be as productive as he'd hoped. The open door might suggest one thing, but Julie's sudden panic over her children had seemed genuine. Perhaps she really had been too ill to think sensibly about keeping the house secure . . . or perhaps she was a better little actress than he'd given her credit for.

He remembered the missing Claire Summers, stage-struck, expensively educated, sexually active teenage rebel. Had she and Julie Garner more in common than their gender? Would Claire, if she was found safe and well, end up having to get married as Julie had done? Would she resent the loss of her ambition as Julie had made clear, on previous occasions, that she did?

Would she see St. Catherine's School and those connected with it as symbols of the chance she had thrown away?

Would she be driven in the end to uttering a cry for help . . . to making some desperate Gesture?

Before his contemplative trance could become pointed, Stone had coaxed Julie to sit down. Would Mrs. Garner— who looked rather on the frail side—like a cup of tea? It wouldn't take long, and she'd feel so much better . . .

"I'd rather have a fag." Julie fumbled with blind hands over the kitchen table. Silently Stone pushed towards her the half-empty cigarette packet and the box of matches. The Garners were indeed short on money: with disposable lighters so cheap, only the very poorest smokers (or those concerned with environmental issues, which in the case of the Garners seemed unlikely) used matches.

The very poorest—who bought clothes from jumble sales because they couldn't afford even charity shop prices. Who, having bought those clothes, cut them to size and sewed them to fit themselves and their children. Sewed them using the hand-cranked machine in its battered plastic case . . .

And unpicked mistakes with a cheap stitch ripper?

Stone looked at Trewley, who had emerged from his trance and was frowning.

"Mrs. Garner," he began, and paused. "Mrs. Garner, there are a few questions we'd like to ask you. . . ."

─────── Twenty-two ───────

STONE'S QUICKER EARS heard it first: the very faintest of footfalls, growing louder as wary feet drew near the door that led from the kitchen to the hall. The eavesdropper couldn't listen at the window, of course: Benson and the young Garners were on duty out in the garden.

Whoever it was must really want to know why the police were so interested in Julie Garner.

Julie, inhaling welcome nicotine, did not notice the approaching intruder. Trewley was preparing to fire his first question—and instead shot an irritated look at Stone. Why hadn't the girl got out her notebook?

He coughed. "Sergeant. To business, if you please." She jumped. He coughed again. "Mrs. Garner, I wonder if you could tell me whether you do much sewing?"

"What the hell *business* of yours is it if I do?"

"We'll take that as yes, Mrs. Garner." Stone was writing it down, all right—but she seemed distracted. What was wrong with the girl? "Sergeant. If you don't mind, Mrs. Garner, are you a good needlewoman?"

"Am I what?"

"Are you clever with your needle? You and your children seem very well dressed. I assume that's because—"

"My kids ain't rubbish, copper! Why shouldn't the poor little bleeders dress smart? They may not be upper-class bitches in posh new uniforms, but I do the best I can for them—which is more than I can say for that bleeding father of theirs. If there's nobody to help me except myself, of course I've got to get clever—right? But what's that to do with anything? I thought you said this was important?"

He hadn't. Was this her guilty conscience putting words into his mouth? "Mrs. Garner—what happens when you make a mistake?"

All she could do was stare at him, her mouth open, the cigarette between her fingers dropping unheeded ash on the check tablecloth.

"Mrs. Garner?"

Her eyes narrowed. "The biggest mistake I made in my life," she told him, "was letting Craig get me up the spout, and believing the bastard when he told me not to get rid of it because he'd look after me. Ha bleeding ha, copper! So what happened then was I had the kid, and two more before I could catch my bleeding breath, and now a fourth on the way—and if I had my time over, that's the last *mistake* I'd make, believe you me!"

She sucked in a furious breath of smoke and burst into a choking fit that had Stone hurrying to the sink for a glass of water.

The sergeant was in no hurry to sit down again. . . .

Trewley looked at her. She was acting so out of character that she must have her reasons. He decided to ignore her: he knew he could trust her.

He hoped.

"Mrs. Garner, I meant mistakes in sewing. When you've gone wrong, how do you unpick your stitches?"

Stone shouted something—dropped her notebook—rushed from kitchen to hall. There came the sound of running feet as she sprinted down the narrow passage and, presumably, out along the front path. . . .

In pursuit of what even the ageing ears of Trewley could hear was another, heavier pair of feet.

Masculine feet.

And Stone, alone, chasing him through the grounds of St. Catherine's School . . .

"Benson!" A pane of glass shattered in the open window. "Get after them!"

And then the bloodhound, baying, was also on the trail.

The fugitive had gained more than a head start, but he—yes, undoubtedly *he*—was heavier in build than the sergeant speeding across the grass in his wake. Not as heavy as the superintendent—not lumbering breathless with the heat, hearing the younger Benson, who'd had to run round the house from the back, coming up fast behind; but still heavier than Detective Sergeant Stone—and more desperate. If the girl caught up with him before the others reached her . . .

The superior should set the example. "Stone!" A gasp. "Wait!" A bellow. "Stop! He can't—get away . . ." *He'd better not. Not before I get there . . .*

"Stone!"

"Sarge!"

The two cries came as one. Benson and Trewley were neck and neck: both could see what was happening as the fugitive, having gained the spinney just ahead of Stone, plunged into the trees and snatched up a fallen branch. He turned to face his pursuers . . .

Who for the first time could see his face.

"Stone!" The superintendent's warning sounded strangely muzzy in his ears. Benson had brushed past him—was blocking his view—was uttering a yell to freeze the blood as he charged to the rescue . . .

Freeze the blood? But his was . . . boiling. Bubbling. Roaring in his ears as his eyes went out of focus and his head began to spin . . .

Superintendent Trewley crashed to the ground, his mind a whirl of arms and legs and looming trees, and sounds of combat that grew slowly fainter . . .

And were silenced, as he plummeted into oblivion.

HE TRIED TO force his eyes open. The lids felt unusually heavy; he was very tired. He gave up the struggle and drifted away, wondering why he felt so full of pins-and-needles—and why he was too sleepy to care.

When he surfaced again, it was to find Stone looking down at him with an expression of anxious relief in her dark eyes. His own eyes—he wanted to rub them, but it was too much of an effort to move his arms—didn't seem to be working properly. There were shadows and shapes where he knew there should be none.

"Floaters," he murmured, for some reason remembering one of his sergeant's little lectures on the mechanics of sight. His own sight must be very far gone for him to see her face looking so . . .

He remembered everything. His eyes flew open. He looked about him and groaned.

"I'm in hospital? What happened?"

"You overdid things," said his sergeant calmly.

"I didn't mean that." Strange how hard it was to find the breath to scold. "As you know very well." Another long breath. "And if you start nagging me, my girl . . . you'll be back in uniform branch before . . ."

He realised that the shadow on her cheek was the darkness of an enormous bruise. "Good God! Are you all right?"

"I'm in better shape than you, sir. You gave us quite a fright. Your wife's hardly speaking to me—she thinks it's all my fault, and," she said as she saw a protest forming on his lips, "Sergeant Pleate has taken what I call really mean advantage of your absence to, um, annexe another interview room. You'd better hurry up and get out of here, you know."

She was pleased to observe how this last intelligence brought the colour back to the sallow cheeks of her superior. She might have been joking about Mrs. Trewley's response to the heat-stroke collapse of her husband, but she'd been far from joking when she said he'd given them all a fright. The doctors had told her that perhaps if she hadn't been there . . .

"Damn Pleate." The ejaculation was halfhearted: there

were, for once, more important things to worry about than Lost Property cupboards. "What the hell happened, Stone? To you, for a start—*and* the rest of it, for pity's sake. If I'm a sick man, you ought to humour me. Think of my blood pressure."

The doctors and dieticians would be talking to him about that later. "Benson's boot's what happened to me, sir. His feet are size twelve. I think I'd have been safer without his kind assistance, to be honest."

"With a maniac charging at you waving a—a bloody great tree? Stop being so damned independent! You could have been killed!"

"Look, sir, I've told you before. The whole point about judo is that you use your opponent's strength and movement against him—so that's what I did. And, to be fair to Benson, his weight came in jolly useful for, um, sitting on the chap while I popped back to take a look at you." No need to dwell on that part. "You looked as if you'd be more comfortable without your tie, so Benson used it instead of handcuffs—oh, yes," she added as the bulldog barked a question. "We got him, all right."

"Did he sing?"

"Eventually, yes." She sighed. "Once we'd found the Summers girl and she started to talk, there wasn't much else he could do."

"Young Claire? She's back? Where was she?"

"Silly little fool," said Stone. "I don't *think* she's realised it yet—she's still in shock—but all three murders were her own stupid fault, in a way. She skipped across to Sayersleigh and checked into a bed-and-breakfast under an assumed name, but the landlady thought there was something a bit fishy about the way she'd arrived without any luggage, and in such an agitated state. When she heard on the local news about the missing schoolgirl, she did the sensible thing and got in touch."

"We never did find out if she'd taken her savings book out of her dad's desk."

"She hadn't."

"Then what did the young idiot hope to do for money? Get a job as a cleaning lady? Go on the game?" Suddenly the look of exasperation he had turned upon his sergeant became a look of dawning horror. "Stone! You don't mean *that's* what this has all been about?"

A sexy, rebellious teenager . . .

"Not quite," said Stone. "But near enough. And if it hadn't been for that new theatre they were so proud of . . . Goodness only knows what Carolyn Armistead will think about it. And perhaps if they hadn't done *Othello*— these lavish costumes, and all that exotic scenery . . . Dirty movies, sir, that's the real story."

He gaped at her. *"Dirty movies?"*

"Pornographic films, if you prefer." Now she'd seen he wasn't going to collapse from shock, she could give him the details. "We know Claire had developed a swollen head about her acting ability and her looks; plus, she was annoyed with her parents—particularly with her father." She tried not to notice the anguished expression on the face of the father of three. It was his right to know, and the doctors said he could take it.

"Well, sir, think how flattered she must have been when a good-looking man of the world paid her compliments and chatted her up as if there was no tomorrow, which at that age there isn't, of course. She was caught up in an affair before she knew what was going on—though I doubt if she would have resisted very hard." Detective Sergeant Stone had done her best to remain impartial, but had found herself decidedly unsympathetic towards the personality of the elder Miss Summers. The fate of the younger sister was never far from the detective's thoughts during the lengthy, tearful interview the girl had insisted on granting without either of her parents present to hear what a mess—not her words, but Stone's—she had made of her life.

"Surprising how many well-brought-up girls have a fancy for a bit of rough trade," said Trewley with a grimace. If any of his three—"So I suppose he flattered her something rotten, got her nicely under his thumb, then told her he had friends—contacts in the business—and she could help herself by being *nice* to people. . . . Ugh!"

"Broadly speaking, sir, yes." She shook her head and sighed. "There's one born every minute, isn't there?"

"Don't remind me! But they're usually innocent young-sters, not the older types. How on earth did Lois Tanner and Brenda French come into it? Did one of 'em make the costumes and the other one slap on the makeup? And you'll never make me believe a nice kid like young Emma—"

"Oh, no, sir. She was as innocent as a baby—and not much older," she added grimly, to drive the hint of tears from her voice. "All she did was spy on Claire and find out roughly what was going on—she thought it was an ordinary affair with a married man—and then she tried to do the brave, decent thing and save her sister's reputation by tackling him about it. I suppose," she mused with some bitterness, "she didn't think it was worth tackling Claire—and she was probably right, from what I've seen of that young lady."

"You didn't like her." It was not a question.

The amateur psychologist shrugged. "It's a fact of life that teenagers are self-centred, to a greater or lesser extent, but Claire's centre is . . . greater than great. I was trying to give her the benefit of the doubt when I said she was still in shock. My candid opinion is that she's far too selfish, as well as too stupid, to realise why all this has happened—and she probably won't, until it all comes out at the trial and her parents learn just what's been going on."

Trewley cocked a knowing eye at her. "Daddy'll tighten the reins, you reckon?"

"Mummy certainly won't. She's . . . devastated over Emma. I don't know when . . ."

"So what about Tanner and French?" demanded Trewley as Stone's voice trailed away. "How did they get involved?"

"Some of this is guesswork, sir . . . but Lois Tanner

saw somebody hanging around the theatre late at night, when she knew there shouldn't have been anyone there. I imagine she was on her way to or from Marianne Gordon's house, keeping an eye on that husband of hers. You remember how the path runs close to the theatre? Perhaps they were careless with the lights—but somehow she knew something was up and made it her business to find out what that something was."

"She was a bossy type, by all accounts. And impetuous. She mightn't have realised what she was getting into."

"I don't suppose she did. It's more benefit-of-the-doubt time now, because she *might* have considered telling the authorities once she found out who appeared to be in charge . . . but then she must have seen the possibilities. She asked for money—the divorce and the breakup of the Stitcherie partnership was going to hit her hard, remember—and he knew she had to be kept quiet. . . ."

"And he kept her. Right. And French?"

"Blackmail again. She'd spotted him fiddling with the pedal control of the sewing machine, and thought nothing of it at first—she wasn't terribly quick, from what everyone says."

"And Garner, being the janitor, had as much right in that room as she had."

"Yes, sir." She glanced at him. "And, um, his own set of keys. Yes," she said as he groaned. "And when the light finally dawned, she was another one who thought she could make money out of what she knew. She made the mistake of getting him to meet her in the needlework room—pointing out the evidence, I suppose—and she didn't see him open the door and slip the treadle belt off the wheel . . ."

"So the stitch ripper, and hiding the body in that bit of shrubbery, really was just a blasted red herring? His smart-arse way of making us think it was the needlework room where the funny goings-on were going on—diverting our attention from the theatre?"

"Um—yes, sir. Of course, once he killed Emma, even

Claire couldn't ignore the possibility that the, um, goings-on had something to do with the murders. She was afraid she'd be his next victim, and she bolted."

"Should have come to us and turned Queen's Evidence," the superintendent growled. "Asked for protection. She's in need of it, all right. Six months in a detention centre and ten years on probation, that's what the daft little madam needs."

"She'll get counselling and social workers, sir." Stone smiled faintly. "Which could be a worse fate, in the end."

"Let's hope so. Pornographic films! Schoolgirls! Talk about corrupting a minor . . ."

"Julie was only fifteen when he got her pregnant," said Stone. "I had him run through the computer. He was lucky not to be done for statutory rape, you know. I *thought* she was rather young to have three children, but it's hard to be sure of ages nowadays. And the poor thing always looked so—so haggard whenever we saw her, it's no surprise we didn't think of checking before."

"Garner's got a taste for young girls?" Trewley's brown eyes gleamed. "He'll have a really tough time inside, and serve the beggar right. And don't tell me about fair play and innocent-until-proved-guilty, because I don't want to know right now. I'm a sick man."

"But improving, sir. So long as you take things easier in future—"

"I told you not to nag! I hate bossy women: and I'll get quite enough of it once I'm home. I don't have to take it from you as well. . . ."

"Talking of bossy women," said Stone as her superior drew a long breath, "Miss Thoday came up with an interesting snippet. She came upon Craig Garner studying the school's master timetable when he'd no business to be doing any such thing. She said she was puzzled by it at the time, but didn't clue up until she realised he must have been finding out when the last class of the day would be using the needlework room. He didn't want to risk electrocuting the wrong person."

"Yes." Trewley shuddered. "Electrocuting the wrong person. How could he be so sure he'd get Tanner and not someone else? It isn't the sort of trick you can pull twice—and surely the beggar wouldn't want a—a practice run at it, would he?"

"Shouldn't think so for one minute, sir. Innocent bystanders only end up dead in the more old-fashioned type of detective fiction." She smiled. "When I had a chance to look through the adult education statements again, the answer was staring me in the face." She smiled again. "Don't tell Sergeant Pleate . . . but it was the electric fan. The janitor was up a ladder fixing the thing when there was that rumpus with Mrs. Pollard about who had the right to use which sewing machine—and Garner heard Lois Tanner staking her claim very, very firmly . . . and—well, Bob's your uncle."

There was a long, thoughtful pause.

Trewley shuddered again.

"Yes," he said, thinking of electricity and the manifold risks attendant upon its use. "That's very . . . perceptive of you, Stone. He was."

He grimaced; and then brightened. "You know, there's a lot to be said for gas. For one thing, you can't run video cameras off it. . . ."

SARAH J. MASON

Sarah J(ill) Mason was born in England (Bishop's Stortford) and went to university in Scotland (St. Andrews). She then lived for a year in New Zealand (Rotorua) before returning to settle only twelve miles from where she started. She now lives about twenty miles outside London with a tame welding engineer husband and two (reasonably) tame Schipperke dogs. Her first (nonseries) mystery, *Let's Talk of Wills*, was published in the United States in 1986.

Sew Easy to Kill is her fifth title featuring Trewley and Stone. Under the pseudonym Hamilton Crane, she has written eleven "Miss Seeton" books in the series created by the late Heron Carvic.